CAL CLARK

GREED

Published by So It Is Written, LLC
Detroit, MI
SoItIsWritten.net

Edited by: So It Is Written – www.SoItIsWritten.net

Formatting: Ya Ya Ya Creative – www.yayayacreative.com

ISBN: 978-0-578-54317-8

LCCN: 2019910041

PRINTED AND BOUND IN THE UNITED STATES OF AMERICA

greed

/grēd/

NOUN

intense and selfish desire for something, especially wealth, power, or food.

CHAPTER 1

It was 8:30 on a Friday night and the parking lot at Ruth's Chris was full. Finding somewhere to park through the plethora of luxury vehicles seemed impossible. Car alarms started going off left and right as Nick cruised through with his speakers on blast in search of an open spot. Nick was infamous in his neighborhood for having the loudest sound system and he had $5,000 in Mickey Shorr receipts to prove it. Cassandra loved the loud music. She loved the way it sent vibrations through her whole body. Shardae, on the other hand, hated it. She hated the fact that it gave her headaches. Every time she got in Nick's car, she couldn't wait to get out.

After the second person came out of the restaurant to make sure their car wasn't being stolen, Nick decided to turn the radio down. He had already gotten two disturbing the peace citations for loud music and he wasn't trying to receive a third. Plus, ever since he put 26-inch rims on his new red Charger, it was screaming, *come indict me.* A flashy car full of black people in a predominantly white neighborhood was a shoo-in for racial profiling, so it was a sigh of relief when he saw a car backing out of a spot.

Nick was glad that he had Cassandra call and make reservations earlier that day. Without reservations on a Friday night, it would be at least a two-hour wait. Over the past year, it became a Friday ritual for Nick and Cassandra to go on a double date with Nate and Shardae. Shardae and Cassandra had been best friends all of their lives, but it wasn't until sophomore year— the year that they both got together with their now boyfriends—that Nick and Nate became "Batman and Robin." Ever since then, the quadruple were inseparable. Nick and Nate scored big with their girlfriends because Cassandra and Shardae were on every guy's "Most Wanted" poster. They were two of the most beautiful girls in the whole city.

Cassandra stood at a mere five foot three inches tall. The sides and back of her head were lightly shaved and she wore the rest of her hair in a red bob that looked fierce against her light complexion. Her freckles would put you under the impression that someone lightly sprinkled nutmeg on her face while she was sleeping. She had the body of a stripper with a butt so big, that you could sit a glass on it.

For her to be so small, she was quite the pugnacious individual. Her mother and father being murdered in front of her when she was four years old in a drug deal gone bad probably had a lot to do with it. She didn't have any family on her father's side. After her parents' deaths, her mother's twin brother inherited the obligation of raising her. Having been raised by a street savvy drug-addicted hustler made her a man's best dream and worst nightmare.

Shardae had more of a swimsuit model built. She had a brown complexion and stood at about five foot seven inches tall with naturally curly hair. Thick black curls draped down her back like curtains and were soft enough to sleep on. Although she wasn't as thick as Cassandra, her body was still banging enough to make Beyoncé take a double glance. Looking at her stomach, one would think that she hadn't eaten any carbohydrates in years. The one quarter of Asian descent that came from her father gave her eyes a slight slant, making her appear to be high even when she wasn't.

Shardae came from a good, middle-class family, but had been estranged from her parents ever since Nate had been released from prison. They gave her the ultimatum of continuing being taken care of and cutting ties with Nate, or continuing to see Nate and cutting ties with her parents. Unfortunately, she chose Nate over her parents. Shortly after, she realized her deplorable decision, but had too much pride to go back. So she had been sticking it out with Nate ever since.

Nick was the pretty boy type. He was six foot five inches tall and weighed a mere 180 pounds with rocks in his pocket. In high school, he was quite the basketball star. In fact, he was ranked 24th in the country until a career-ending knee injury sent his hoop dreams down the drain. Despite him coming from a good family, he had some type of street nostalgia that would end up inhibiting him for the rest of his life. Afraid of being judged for his bad decisions, he ostracized himself from his family and turned to the streets for everything that he needed.

Nick and Nate were complete opposites in looks and personality. Nate stood at five feet eight inches and was 200 pounds of all muscle via his three-year prison tenure. He had a dark complexion and long dreadlocks that made him look Jamaican. His mother was a prostitute who was murdered by a John while he was still in diapers. He never knew who his father was. He spent most of his childhood year in and out of foster homes and detention centers. By age 16, he was a full-time drug dealer and quite the formidable one at that. Shardae, Nick and Cassandra were the only family that he had.

Heads turned as the quad made their way through the restaurant to be seated at their table. Despite them frequenting the restaurant, they still looked and felt out of place. Maybe it was the jewelry, dread locks and tattoos. Or it could've been the marijuana stench reeking from them that was strong enough to give the whole restaurant a contact high. Either way, they could tell that most of the people eating felt uncomfortable by their presence. The quad ordered their usual, which coincidently was filet mignon and baked potato, and began to chow down.

"You know you gotta have your money ready for tomorrow, bro?" Nick said reminding Nate of their four kilogram shipment that they were supposed to be getting tomorrow.

"I'm a have it ready. Same price, right?" Nate asked.

"Yup, same price, bro."

"See dog, that's why we need a new connect. I'm tired of fuckin wit Fred's tight ass."

"Isn't that Fred right there?" Shardae asked, pointing at booth across the restaurant.

"Yeah, that's him." Nick said, squinting his eyes to get a better look. "That's him and Diego with two girls."

"Man, fuck Fred!" Nate interrupted. "That nigga lucky you're cool with him or I'd a been took all of his shit. He got all of them high ass prices on that dope. The only reason he's even getting some money is because that Mexican bitch daddy fronted him all that dope and then died."

"Babe, why don't you all just try to buy more and see if he'll give it to you for a cheaper price?" Shardae suggested.

"Why don't you just shut yo' fuckin' mouth and stay out of my business affairs!" Nate snapped.

"Unt unn, why the fuck you gotta talk to her like that?!" Cassandra snapped, waving her index finger in Nate's face.

"Nick, you betta get yo mothafuckin' girl, dog."

"Nigga, you got me fucked up. Can't nobody get me!" Cassandra snapped, starting to make a scene.

"Whoa, whoa, whoa! Y'all chill that shit out! We trying to have a good time. Everybody need to just enjoy their meals and chill," Nick said peacefully.

"You know what? I done lost my appetite. I'm going to the bathroom and then we can go," Cassandra said pushing her plate in front of her before getting up from the table.

"Hold on, I'm coming, too," Shardae said as she got up to follow.

Before the girls were able to make it to the bathroom, they were slowed down by a familiar voice.

"Damn girl, what's yo' name?"

They both turned to put a face to the very familiar voice. They both started smiling once they saw it was Fred. They were so upset that they forgot they had to past Fred's table in order to get to the bathroom. As Fred stood up to greet them, they were both in awe of how good he looked. They had all known each other since high school, but it had been almost a year since that last time they had all seen each other. Fred was about five foot seven inches tall and had a very athletic built. He had a light complexion, thick wavy hair and wore a full beard light enough to have been shaded in with a #2 pencil.

Fred had a crush on Shardae since high school, and that was the main reason why Nate didn't like him. Ever since they had known Fred, he had been very flamboyant. At the very moment, he was wearing enough jewelry to make you think he was a drug dealer or a rapper. Coincidently, he was both.

"I ain't seen y'all in forever. How y'all doing?" Fred asked as he hugged Cassandra.

"Fine," Shardae and Cassandra both said in unison.

Fred then gave Shardae a hug and whispered in her ear, "When you gone let me make you my girlfriend?"

He could tell that she was flattered by her ear to ear smile, but ignoring his question she politely shot back, "Are you going to introduce us to y'alls girlfriends?"

"Well ahh, actually these are friends of some friends who are in from Mexico. We're just showing them a good time until they leave tomorrow. This is Selma and this is Roslyn. And don't either of them speak English too good," Fred said smiling.

Both of the women at the table were absolutely gorgeous. Selena had long, blonde wavy hair with green eyes that gave her a Caribbean look. The other girl Roslyn had more of a tan color that really offset her long black hair. Both of them had full sets of lips and boobs so big that you couldn't tell if they were real or not.

"What about him, he can't speak English either?" Cassandra asked pointing at the other man seated at the table.

"My bad," Fred apologized. "This is my main man, Diego. Diego, this is Shardae and Cassandra."

"Hey," Cassandra and Shardae both said in unison.

"What's happenin' shawty?" Diego said, smiling exposing a mouth full of gold teeth.

Diego was a brown complexioned younger guy who happened to be a gang member and hitman from Mississippi. He came to Michigan to do some dirty work for Fred. To make a long story short, Fred was so pleased with his work that he moved him up here permanently, giving him the job as his personal bodyguard.

"Listen, I'm having a party this weekend. Call me tomorrow and I'll give y'all some VIP passes. Y'all can even bring the hubbies," Fred said laughing.

"Alright, we'll call you." They could see Nick and Nate staring at them so they hurried to the bathroom and make their way back to their table.

"What the fuck was that?" Nate asked irately.

"Nothing," Shardae pleaded. "He just invited the four of us to his party this weekend."

"Man, fuck that party! I ain't going and you ain't going either!" The more belligerent Nate became, the more people started to stare to see what was going on.

"C'mon bro, chill out. Let's just get out of here," Nick suggested in hopes of eradicating the scene that Nate was making. "Umm, excuse me, can we get our check please?" Nick asked flagging down the waiter.

The waiter approached the table with a bottle in hand.

"Actually sir, the gentlemen over there," the waiter said, pointing to Fred's table, "took the liberty of paying your bill and sending over this bottle of Penfolds Grange 2007."

"Bottle of what?" Nick asked.

"It's a $900 bottle of wine, sir."

"Man, who the fuck does this nigga think he is?" Nate asked rhetorically. "Send that shit back and we'll pay for our own mothafuckin' food."

"Let me take care of this," Nick pleaded. "I got this; y'all can go to the car and I'll meet y'all out there."

Nate and Shardae continued to argue all the way to the car. Fred saw all of the commotion and gave Nick the "what's going on?" look. Nick shrugged his shoulders and put his fist up to his ear with his thumb and pinky finger extended to let Fred know that he'd call him later. Nick then paid their bill and headed to the parking lot. He could hear someone's car alarm system screaming for help. He made it just in time to impede on what was now turning into a physical altercation.

"Bitch, if I find out you fuckin him, I'm killing you and that nigga!" Nate yelled as he grabbed Shardae by the throat, pushing her up against someone else's car.

"Let her go!" Cassandra screamed as she tried grabbing Nate's hand from her best friend's throat.

Nate's attention was now drawn toward Cassandra. He clinched his fist and jumped at her as if he were about to punch her.

"I wish you would put your hands on me," Cassandra taunted.

All of a sudden, Nick lunged in front of Cassandra as if to block her from the ensuing punch.

"Dog, you betta get yo' bitch," Nate warned while pointing his finger at Cassandra

"I got yo' bitch; you bitch ass nigga!" Cassandra shot back.

"What the fuck is wrong with you, bro? You out here trippin' for no reason. All Fred was doing was inviting us to his party. You got these people's car alarms going off and shit. You gone have us going to jail out here."

The owner of the silver Escalade truck who happened to be a young Arabic man wearing an all-white Keffiyeh ran out to see why his alarm was going off.

"Hey, hey!" the man yelled. "Get the hell away from my car before I call the cops!"

"Come on y'all! Let's get the fuck out of here before we all go to jail," Nick suggested as he rushed them all to the car.

Diego could tell that something was bothering Fred because he hadn't said a word since Nate had stormed out of the restaurant.

"What's up man? You straight bruh?" Diego asked.

"Yeah, I'm straight like a perm. I just hope I don't have to kill this clown ass nigga."

"All you gotta do is say the word bruh, and I'll knock all the meat out that nigga taco."

"Naw, not yet at least. We just wait it out, play the situation cool and see what happens."

CHAPTER 2

It was about 12:30 in the afternoon and the birds were chirping nonstop as if they had all hung out the night before and came back with stories to tell. The floor to ceiling picture windows in Nick and Cassandra's two-bedroom apartment allowed the sun's bright rays to illuminate their living room. Piles of money were scattered across the living room floor. To make more room, Nick had to move the coffee table from its original spot and sit it adjacent to the window.

Looking at all of the money on the floor made him feel like he was in a scene from the movie, *Paid In Full*. Like many other urban youths, the money is what kept him going. The money is what gave him the rush; it gave him some type of euphoric feeling that was indescribable. Nick was never considered to be a formidable figure when it came to the streets, so he tried to make up for it in other areas like hustling. At the end of the day, all Nick was known for was hustling, and he was content with that. He was content with his upscale lifestyle and beautiful girlfriend, who had an attitude with him ever since they left the restaurant last night. Even though Nate gave everyone one of the sincerest apologies, it was still plenty of tension.

Cassandra was sick and tired of Nick and Nate. She was tired of Nate acting like a jealous, controlling asshole and treating her best friend like shit. And she was tired of Nick acting so timid. Honestly, she didn't want to hear from or speak to either one of them for at least another two days, but right now, she didn't have much of a choice. Nate had just dropped his half of the money for the four kilograms of cocaine that they were about to buy and she had to help Nick count it. It didn't take much for her to swallow her pride, be a good girlfriend and help him count it because she knew that a Neiman Marcus shopping spree was imminent.

"San! San!" Nick yelled loud enough for everyone in the 75-unit apartment building to hear.

"Here I come, dang."

"I asked you to get me some rubber bands out of the drawer, not from Mexico."

"Don't rush me," Cassandra said as she entered the room, throwing a pack of rubber bands on Nick's lap.

As Cassandra pranced her bare feet across the floor, her perfectly pedicured toes sunk into the carpet with every step she took. The frosty air blowing from the air conditioner sent a slight chill through her body, making her nipples erect. The tips of her areolas protruded through her small white tank top, making it look like she had rifle bullets in her shirt. Her tight boxer briefs hugged her body like spandex.

"What's in this bag?" Cassandra asked, kicking the red duffle bag that sat on the floor.

Before she could reach down to grab it, Nick snapped out of his daydream and grabbed it.

"This ain't nothing. Just something that I have to drop off to my homeboy," Nick responded as he picked the bag up and threw it onto the kitchen floor.

"I don't know why we have to count this money in the first place. Didn't dumb ass count it before he brought it over here?"

"Yeah he did, but we still have to count it again because if it's short, then I have to pay for it."

Nick had known Nate far too long for him not to double check his money. Although they had been friends for years, Nate was still a shady individual who wouldn't hesitate to get down. And for some reason, Nick somehow always seemed to feel the wrath of Nate's shadiness. It was like Nate had worked out some type of sinister deal with karma that made him exempt. He had somehow figured out a way to outwit the laws of human nature, because he always did bad things without anything bad ever being reciprocated. And to top it off, Nick knew that Nate despised Fred.

There were rumors going around about a clandestine liaison between Fred and Shardae while Nate was incarcerated. Although it had never been proven, Nate was a pessimist and he knew that Fred was a well-known philanderer with a lot of money. Naturally, Shardae denied the accusations; without any solid evidence other than hearsay, he had to give her the benefit of the doubt. Thus far, Nate had yet to do anything shady with the money that they had to pay Fred, but Nick still always double checked.

"San, make sure that it is $1,000 in each stack of money. It should be 40 of them all together."

Cassandra's fingers began to hurt after about 10 minutes of counting. Despite her feeling like she had caught arthritis, she somehow managed to finish, using her shopping spree as motivation. By the time she had finished, Nick had counted his portion twice.

Nick was elated because this was going to be the most drugs that he and Nate had ever bought. Their plan was to go to Ohio, where the drugs sold for twice as much, and set up shop. If everything went as planned, they'd both bring back six figures a piece.

"Oohh wee!" Nick shouted with a joker smile on his face. "I'm about to be *ballin'*!"

"And I'm about to be *shopping!*" Cassandra yelled even louder with an even bigger smile on her face. "Neiman Marcus, here I come!"

"Well, I sure hope you got some Neiman Marcus money."

"Boy, please. All the dope my boyfriend sells, I'll be damned if I don't look good," Cassandra shot back as stood up and sashayed back and forth across the room like she was auditioning to be on America's Next Top Model.

"C'mere," Nick said softly.

Cassandra walked over and stood between his legs as he sat on the sofa.

"Baby, you gone always look good as long as you mine. I'm gone always keeps you shopping at Neiman Marcus," Nick said as he slid her shirt up in the front just enough to kiss her navel.

"Stop, not right now." Cassandra whined.

Nick's kisses began to travel from her navel where her diamond studded heart-shaped belly ring was to her crotch. He could feel the barbell piercing in her clitoris pressing up against his top lip as he kissed her through her boxer briefs. Her love box began to moisten profusely as he blew his warm breath on it through her shorts. With every kiss, her goodies became warmer and warmer as if her shorts could potentially catch fire. Nick started to feel the moisture on his lips as the juices started to seep through the fabric.

"Oooh Nick!"

She could no longer resist. Before she knew it, she was lying on her back, helping Nick help her out of her shorts. She grabbed her feet and held her legs open as wide as they could go while Nick buried his face in her crotch. As Nick stuck his middle finger inside of her in search of her G-spot, her panting became longer and louder, reminiscent of a thirsty puppy. He could tell when she was climaxing because she started screaming louder and secretion began to squirt on his chin, running down his hand like a waterfall. He tried to ingest all of the fluid coming out of her, but it was too much for him. The juices started to run down her butt cheeks, allowing the carpet to absorb the excess amount. She let out a last sigh of relief while he used his tongue to clean her up. Nick unzipped his pants exposing his fully erect tool and before he could insert it into her, she jumped up, grabbing her shorts off the floor.

"What you doin'? Where you goin'?" Nick asked with a puzzled look on his face and his genitals still in his hand.

"I'm going to get in the shower 'cause I have a few runs to make."

"But hold on! You just gone leave me like this?"

Cassandra walked up close to him and grabbed his rod. She could feel the blood still pumping through it as she softly kissed him on the lips. "You might get lucky later on, so don't stay out all night. I love you and be careful."

She walked in the bathroom and closed the door. Nick thought that this was some sort of joke until he heard the shower water turn on. He went to turn the knob on the bathroom door and it was locked. He couldn't believe what had just happened; he didn't know what to say or do. All of a sudden, he heard the water being turned off and saw the bathroom door open.

"Don't forget your gun from on top of the refrigerator! Love you!" She yelled before slamming the door and cutting the water back on.

"Ain't this about a bitch?" Nick said to himself and he fixed his clothes and grabbed the two bags. He knew that she was still mad at him about last night, but he didn't think that she would take it this far. At least she did remind him about his gun because he had completely forgot. Being in the streets, it was a must to carry a pistol. Even if you didn't plan on using it, you still wanted people to think that you would because it was no telling what might happen. Nick grabbed his pistol and headed out to meet Fred.

Drug paraphernalia was scattered all over Tony Boy's room. Anyone who walked in could tell that a drug addict stayed there. His full-sized mattress laid on the floor in the corner of the room. There was no headboard or box spring, just a mattress with sheets that hadn't been changed in only God knows when. Tony Boy was confined to one side of the mattress because the springs on the other side were beginning to protrude through the mattress. The springs were sharp enough to cut you.

His 13-inch television sat on a milk crate on the floor. The antenna was missing, so a dinner fork had to be attached to the back of the TV in order for a picture to show. Sitting next to an ashtray on the floor was a dinner plate that contained drug crumbs, a syringe and a razor blade. The location of the only electrical outlet in the room forced an extension cord to wrap around Tony Boy's bed like an anaconda. Due to the shortage in the cord, silver electrical tape was wrapped around it, making it resemble a mummy. The slightest touch would make the TV cut off.

Despite not having any natural light coming in, the room was lit up like a Christmas tree. A heavy wool blanket was nailed to the window, blocking the slightest bit of sun from peaking in. The primary source of light came from an old lamp sitting on the floor whose lamp shade had been M.I.A. for years. Although the lamp was designed to hold a 60-watt light bulb, it held a 100-watt bulb that got hot enough to light a cigarette. The secondary source of light came from a lighter whose metal backing had been dismembered, making the flame shoot up far enough to burn off Tony Boy's eyebrows. He twirled the pipe through the flames with his thumb and index finger, taking long hard puffs of the crack rock.

As the smoke he inhaled traveled through his blood stream, his brain began releasing high levels of dopamine all at once. For about 30 seconds, the feeling of utopia took over his whole body from head to toe, followed by an urgent sense of paranoia. He slowly walked over to the hanging wool blanket. He nervously peeked through the window as if he were playing hide and seek and to be found meant he would die. His paranoia soon turned into obsessive compulsion. He began to pick up anything off the floor that resembled cocaine. After putting several items in his mouth, none of which emulating the numbing taste of cocaine, he decided to give it a rest.

Tony Boy was about five foot four inches tall and weighed a mere 110 pounds. He normally kept his face completely nude to try to keep his youth; but he hadn't shaved in days and the stubbles were starting to poke through. Years of drug abuse and lack of sleep put dark bags and heavy wrinkles under the eyes of his light complexioned face. Tony Boy had a really good grade of hair that he wore in a wavy pony tail that stretched to his shoulders.

His problems began to surface as his high started to go down. Butch had just left to go to the store and would be back in any minute now. Tony Boy had just smoked the last of his dope. He had given him specific instructions before he left to only smoke two rocks and to leave the remaining three for him. The only reason Butch didn't take his dope with him to the store is because he was already on the run. If he got caught, he didn't want to catch a dope case to go along with his list of pending charges. So with blatant disregard for Butch's wishes, Tony Boy smoked all of his dope. Now he knew it was going to be a problem when Butch got back. But in his eyes, it was all Butch's fault. Addicts are only loyal to their vices and Butch should've known better. Plus, Nick and Nate were on their way to cook up some drugs at the house, which meant free samples. For some odd reason, Nick wanted Butch to be there and he being there was just another set of lungs to smoke up the free samples. So Tony Boy wanted to be one up on him and by smoking all of his dope, he did just that. He froze as Butch walked through the door singing his own remix version of a song that he had just heard.

"'Bout to smoke two rocks at da same damn time. Smoke a square and a rock at da same damn time," Butch sang. Butch stood at the doorway of Tony Boy's room wearing a pair of dirty cargo shorts and a flannel shirt that was unbuttoned, exposing the hair on his abdomen. He was a very pudgy guy, standing at a mere five foot six inches tall and weighting around 190 pounds which he carried mostly in his stomach. His shoes looked as if he just finished cutting grass and had an egregious smell coming from them. It may've been because Butch wasn't wearing any socks or because he had really just got done cutting grass; but either way, they smelled horrible.

"Pass me that straight shooter," Butch pointed in reference to the crack pipe sticking out of the pocket on Tony Boy's shirt. "So I can smoke two rocks at the same damn time." Butch continued to sing as he began to shrug his shoulders up and down in some sort of dance move.

"Listen Bay Boy…" Tony Boy began to explain.

"Listen my ass! I know you still betta have my shit."

"Just hold on a second and listen bay boy. Nah, I smoked all the dope but—"

"You a got damn lie!" Butch interrupted. "I know good and got damn well you ain't smoked all my shit!"

"Listen Bay Boy, just listen. My nephews Lil' Nicky and Nate are on they way over here now to cook up a bunch of shit. And Lil' Nicky told me to make sure you was here cause he had something for you."

"You a got damn lie, Tony Boy. You a got damn lie!" Butch shouted belligerently with both fists clinched as if he were about to throw a punch.

"Keep it down Bay Boy for you wake my daddy up."

"Naw, nigga! Fuck that! I'm 'bout to whoop yo ass!" Butch shouted.

As both men squared off, they both began flinching at each other back and forth, putting any potential spectators under the impression that either man knew whether to throw or to expect a punch.

"Come on Bay Boy, hit me. Hit me!" Tony Boy taunted. "Nigga, I wish you would hit me! I swear to God you bet not hit me."

"Oh, I'm finna hit you, mothafucka!" Butch shouted, swinging a haymaker punch that missed the intended target by about a foot.

Tony Boy almost punched himself as he threw both arms up trying to duck and block the punch at the same time.

"Nigga, I wish you woulda hit me, Bay Boy. I wish you mothafuckin' woulda!" Tony Boy taunted as they squared off again.

"Come on nigga; come on!" Butch yelled, swinging and missing yet another punch.

"Yeah, you betta miss nigga!" Tony Boy yelled almost falling trying to block a punch that never came.

All of a sudden, the "fight" for lack of better term was broken up by a knock at the door. Both men froze to see who it was.

"See Bay Boy! I told you they was coming! I told you! We both finna smoke two rocks at the same damn time." Tony Boy said smiling, trying to get a reading on Butch to see if he was going to let him through the doorway.

"Mothafucka, you shol' betta hope that's them, or yo' ass nigga."

"Nigga, you bet not hit me. I ain't no hoe Bay Boy," Tony Boy said, flinching and ducking as he slid pass Butch to answer the door.

CHAPTER 3

Cassandra had just gotten dressed so she was looking and feeling really good. It wasn't even 2:00 yet, and she had already received some oral pleasures resulting in an orgasm, so thus far, her day was going great. She had just picked up a flyer for Fred's party at the store and decided to drop by Shardae's house to see if she wanted to go. Plus, she wanted to make sure that Shardae was alright because she hadn't talked to her since last night. Nick and Nate were going to be in Ohio for at least a full day, so she wanted to try to seize the opportunity and try to persuade Shardae into going. The truth was that despite them all being friends since high school, she was starting not to like Nate. She would much rather her friend be in a relationship with Fred, but she knew how crazy Nate was, so she knew that it was much easier said than done. Shardae was sitting on her apartment patio, drinking a glass of wine when Cassandra pulled up.

"Damn bitch, you getting started early ain't you?" Cassandra asked referring to the drink in her hand.

"Girl, after last night, I needed a drink."

"He didn't put his hands on you, did he?" Cassandra asked as she sat her purse down and began to visibly examine her face.

"Girl, naw. When y'all dropped us off last night, he just kept apologizing. He knows better than to put his hands on me. We may have tussled before a few times, but he has never hit me. And every time he calls his self showing out, I make him take me shopping. In fact, I made him promise to take me to the Gucci store when they come back from Ohio. And he won't be getting any coochie until I get my Gucci," Shardae said laughing as she held her hand up pointing her index finger down towards her lap.

"I'm making Nick take me shopping, too!" Cassandra said laughing as she slapped Shardae's hand with a high five. "And before he left this morning, he gave me some head and I got straight up and got in the shower and left him there looking stupid."

"Unt unn!? He went down on you and you didn't even give him none?" Shardae asked in disbelief.

"Nope."

Shardae and Cassandra both burst out laughing and slapped each other high fives. Now that the mood had lightened up a bit, this was the perfect time for Cassandra to inquire about Fred's party.

"Look whose party flyer I just got," Cassandra said as she rummaged through her purse.

Shardae broke a smile as she grabbed the flyer. She carefully examined it without saying a word.

"Soooo, what do you think? You wanna go?"

"Girl, I don't know. Nate would have a heart attack if he found out. You saw how he acted last night."

"Fuck Nate, Day Day! You need to leave his ass alone anyways. Plus you know Fred has been trying to get with you for years."

"Well for one, we both know that Fred is a player and for two, you know I just can't leave Nate. You know that man is crazy."

"You could at least go to the party with me. I know you're not going to make me go by myself. Please Day Day, pleeease," Cassandra begged.

"I'll think about it." Shardae replied smiling. "Think!"

Cassandra gave her a big hug and they both walked into her apartment.

Nate stood on Tony Boy's front porch ringing the doorbell hysterically. His patience was wearing thin because Tony Boy knew that he was on his way over. The screen door was locked, but the front door was cracked enabling Nate to hear all of the commotion. His clairvoyant pessimism began to kick in as he clutched his pistol off his hip.

"Hey hey! I'm coming Bay Boy. I hear ya!" Tony Boy yelled as he unlocked the screen door, sweating and breathing hard with a huge welcoming smile on his face.

"Man, what the fuck do you got goin on in here? You look like you just got into a fight. Are you straight?" Nate asked as he cocked his Uzi and loaded a bullet into the chamber.

"Naw naw! Everything cool Bay Boy. I just put my daddy to sleep and I got the kitchen all cleaned up for you boys."

"Who the fuck do you got in here with you?"

"Aw that ain't nobody; it's just my main man, Butch."

"Butch? What the fuck is Butch doin' here?!" Nate asked with one eyebrow raised. "You know what we came here to do."

"I already know Bay Boy. But when Lil' Nicky called me, ya understand, he told me to make sure Butch was here. He said something about he wanted Butch to check something out or something."

"Ain't that about a bitch? He wanted Butch to check something out?" Nate asked rhetorically "He ain't been having Butch check nothing out."

"That's the same thing I said, Bay Boy. But hold on a minute so I can go and get him," Tony Boy said as he walked to his room in the back of the house. "Nigga, I told you that my nephews was on the way. That's one of them out there now. Come on nigga; we finna get high as a fur coat."

"'Bout time they got here nigga 'cause I'm ready to smoke—"

"Ssshhh!" Tony Boy interrupted as he put his index finger on his lips. "Just be cool Bay Boy, just be cool."

Nate was hanging up his cell phone as Butch and Tony Boy walked into the living room. He then adjusted the gun that was now on his hip to let Butch know that he was armed.

"Butch, you 'member by nephew Nate? Nate, you 'member my main man, Butch?"

"Hey hey! What's up Nate?" Butch said as he extended his hand out for a hand shake.

"Ain't shit up!" Nate stated firmly with his arms still at his sides, refusing the handshake. "Hey Tony Boy. Nick should be pulling up shortly, so I need you to go to the store and get two boxes of baking soda, a pack of Backwoods, and a two-liter grape Faygo." Nate pulled a $50 bill from out of his pocket and handed it to Tony Boy. "Hurry up before Nick gets here and bring back all of my change."

"Damn, Bay Boy! Buy me a brew. I don't want nothin' but a double deuce. Look out for me one time," Tony Boy begged.

"Go ahead man, gotdamn!"

"Good lookin' out Bay Boy, good lookin'," Tony Boy said as he headed for the door.

"Hold on Tony Boy. That bitch Tina owe me $8. I'm a walk around there with you to see if I can catch her."

"Naw, hold up homeboy," Nate said as he stepped in front of the door blocking Butch's exit. "I don't know you and I damn shol' don't trust you, so you ain't goin' nowhere. You stayin' right here wit me."

Butch was speechless. He had already become terrified of Nate and he hadn't been there for 20 minutes yet. Nate had a monstrous aura about himself and that's the way he liked it.

With nothing else to do, Butch looked up at Tony Boy for some sort of recourse.

"It's cool, Bay Boy. It's cool. I'll be right back."

Lying on the other side of Tony Boy's house was a 10-speed bike that looked like it belonged to an eight-year old girl. The bike was pink and white and had matching ribbons coming out of the handles on the handle bars. Not only did the bike have a loose seat, but it didn't have any brakes so you had to stop with your foot. Tony Boy felt like a modern-day Flintstone riding this bike, but he didn't care because today was his lucky day. He knew that he was minutes away from getting high as a kite, so he hopped on the bike and proceeded to the liquor store.

CHAPTER 4

Nick pulled up on the block and awaited Fred's arrival. They had just got off the phone and he was only minutes away. After meeting Fred, Nick was supposed to meet up with Nate at Tony Boy's house so they could cook their drugs up and head to Ohio. Nick was beginning to look at Nate as an inconvenience. Every time they got ready to buy more drugs, he had to meet with Fred alone because there was so much tension between the two of them. It was hard for him to understand Nate's dislike for Fred because he didn't like him enough to hang out with him or go to his parties, but he didn't mind buying drugs from him. By Nick being the person in the middle, he tried his best to keep the tension down because he knew that if it wasn't for him, Nate and Fred would have already tried to kill each other a long time ago.

As far as he was concerned, Nate was jealous of Fred. His whole train of thought was broken when he heard a sound that mimicked a school bus. He looked up and saw that it was Fred in a white Chevy dually truck. The truck was massive and it had to be new because it had a paper plate in the window. He grabbed the book bag with the $80,000 in it and got in the truck with Fred.

"What up doe?" Fred said as he extended his hand to give Nick a handshake.

"Nothin' bro, just chillin'," Nick said as he shook Fred's hand. "Me and Nate about to take this shit down to Ohio but we'll be back in a few days."

"Dog, what's up with that nigga Nate?" Fred asked in reference to the incident that took place last night. "I don't want to have to get his brains knocked out."

"Aw bro, it ain't even nothing like that. Dude was just drunk and started tripping for no reason. You already know if it was something like that, I would've let you know. That's my man and all, but you and me go all the way back to elementary school."

"Alright cool. I just wanted to make sure."

Nick unzipped the book bag and opened it up wide enough for Fred to see all of the stacks of money. Fred zipped the book bag back up and nonchalantly threw it on the back seat without even counting it. He then grabbed a Foot Locker bag off the backseat floor and handed it to Nick. The contents of the bag were four kilos of cocaine wrapped in layers of silver electrical tape. Nick picked up one of the kilos and examined it before throwing it back in the bag.

"You straight?" Fred asked.

"Yep."

"Listen dog, I'm about to start fuckin' with this rap shit full time, so after I'm through with this last shipment, I'm done. You gone have to start fuckin' with my man, Diego. So save up all of your money and when y'all get done with these four bricks, bring me a $100,000 and I'll give you 10 bricks and you can owe me $100,000," Fred explained.

"Alright bro, bet. That's good looking out. I'm a call you as soon as we get done."

The two of them slapped hands one last time before parting ways. Over the years, Fred had took a liking to

Nick. But Nate, on the other hand, he couldn't stand and if need be, his demise was just a phone call away. His train of thought was broken by his cell phone ringing. He grabbed his cell phone off his lap and saw that it was Carlos.

"Carlos, what's going on?"

"Nothing much my friend. How are you?" Carlos asked with a strong Spanish accent.

"I'm good, how about you?"

"Excellent my friend, excellent. Did you receive the shipment?"

"Yep, I got it yesterday."

"Excellent, so I'll be expecting the money by next week. I'll call you back to check on everything in 72 hours."

"Alright, cool." Fred said trying to rush him off the phone.

"Good bye, my friend."

Nick pulled around the corner to Tony Boy's house and saw Nate's car out front, so he knew that he was inside waiting. Nick took a deep breath and said a quick prayer before walking in the house. Nate had been making Butch feel uncomfortable the whole time that he was there, so he was very excited to see Nick walk in the door.

"What' up boyay?" Butch greeted Nick as he walked in the door.

"Shit, what's up bro?"

"Damn nigga, it took you long enough!" Nate snapped impatiently.

"Yeah, I know. Fred was talking my head off. Where's Tony Boy?"

"I just sent him to the store, but he should be on his way back by now. But let me holler at you in the kitchen for a minute." Nate requested, still wanting to know why Butch was over there in the first place.

"Hold on bro; I gotta answer this. It's Fred," Nick said as he picked up his phone. "Hello?"

"Aye dog, it's about four police cars comin' up towards your way right now."

"They're coming this way?" Nick asked.

"Yeah. I don't know if they're comin' exactly to where you at, but they definitely coming your way."

"Alright, good lookin' out bro."

"Yup, yup!"

Nick hung up the phone to inform Nate of what was going on, but the volume of his phone was up high enabling Nate to hear everything that was said.

Paranoia was written all over Nate's face despite his best endeavor to hide it. Years ago, he had made a promise to himself that he would die before ever going back to prison and had every intention of keeping that promise. He lit up a Newport cigarette to try to calm his nerves.

"Just relax, bro," Nick said trying to keep Nate at ease. "It's a million houses on this street. Why would they be coming here?" He asked rhetorically.

"Yeah, you right. All Tony Boy do is get high. Why would the police be fuckin' with him for?" As Nate walked to peek through the blinds, he could see Tony Boy hitting the corner so hard that the chain on the bike slipped, causing him to fall. After tumbling several times, he got up and proceeded to run full speed as if he was being chased. Nate could see three police cars hit the corner behind him.

"It's the motha' fuckin' police!" Nate yelled as he dropped the lit cigarette on the floor.

Before anyone could respond to Nate's comment, Tony Boy burst in the door, yelling hysterically.

"Get rid of the shit Bay Boy! Whatever ya got, hide it 'cuz they comin'!"

Water glistened off Maria's body like honey as she got out of the bath tub. She stood at five foot one, and weighed only 105 pounds. Her narcissism began to emerge as she walked past the full-sized mirror in her bedroom. Lying in the sun nude for an hour had given her body the perfect tan. The Atlanta sun wasn't nothing compared to the one back home in Mexico, but it still got the job done. Maria's greenish hazel eyes accentuated her beach sand complexion perfectly. Her long silky black hair draped down her back, making her look like a close relative of Pocahontas. The beauty mark that was stationed above the top corner of her mouth was sexy enough to make Cindy Crawford jealous. There wasn't a blemish on her body, putting you under the impression that she had never fallen off a bicycle before. A thin line of black hair started inches below her belly button and trailed down to her plump lips that hung just enough for you to see them from behind her.

Looking at herself in the mirror made her feel like she was perfect, and she knew that it wasn't many people that would disagree. As she got the lotion off the dresser and began to moisturize her body, she started to get turned on. The size of her peach-colored areolas changed from quarters to silver dollars in seconds. It had been almost two weeks since the last time she had sex, and she was well overdue. One of her girlfriends had bought her a sex toy that vibrates in unison with the sound of music. Today seemed like the perfect time to use it. As she laid her flawless body across the 1,000-count Egyptian sheets, her moment of self-gratification was broken up before it even began. Her levels of irritability began to rise with each ring that her phone sung. She smacked her lips as she reached for her phone, but immediately started smiling once she saw who it was.

"Hi, baby!" Maria answered on the fourth ring.

"What's up babe; how are you?"

"I'm fine. How are you?"

"You already know, I'm alright like a A-plus paper."

"That's good," Maria responded with a huge smile.

"Well look baby, I didn't want anything. I just thought about you and wanted to call to hear your voice."

"Awww, that is so sweet, and I was just thinking about you too, babe. Listen, I was going to surprise you, but I'm just going to tell you. In two days, I'm flying out to see you."

There was an awkward silence that lasted for about five seconds.

"Soooo," Maria said, breaking the awkward silence. "Are you happy?"

"Yeah, of course I'm happy. I can't wait to see you."

"Then it's a date. I'll call you when my plane takes off so you can pick me up from the airport, okay?"

"Alright baby, I love you."

"Okay, love you too babe, bye."

CHAPTER 5

Nate's jaws dropped as he took a glimpse out of the window. Pulling in front of Tony Boy's house were three police cars along with one that was unmarked. Nate didn't have a clue what was going on, but he knew that whatever it was couldn't be good.

"All shit!" Nate yelled as he pulled out his Uzi. "I ain't goin' back to jail!"

"Hold on Bay Boy; be cool," Tony Boy said in hopes of calming Nate down.

"Fuck this. I got to get the fuck up out of here. I'm on the run," Butch said as he stood up in an attempt to make an escape.

Nate pointed his loaded gun close enough to Butch's face that he could've kissed the barrel. "Man, sit cho' bitch ass down! You ain't goin' nowhere!"

"C'mon bro, chill out," Nick pleaded.

"Just be cool, Bay Boy," Tony Boy joined in.

"Everybody shut the fuck up!" Nate yelled waving the loaded machine gun in all of their direction.

Boom! Boom! Boom!

"Police, open up!"

Boom! Boom! Boom!

"It's the police, open up!"

Nate stood on the other side of the door with his weapon drawn as if he were about to eradicate the entire police force. Nick began to panic as the reality of their plight began to set in. Beads of sweat began to roll down his face like bowling balls as his anxiety made him perspire. He could feel his heart rate and blood pressure shooting to the sky. The whole ambience of the house had turned deadly in a matter of seconds. Nick knew that he had to do something and he had to do it fast. From out of nowhere, an ounce of courage struck his body like a bolt of lightning. Nick ran into the kitchen and cut on all four eyes of the stove as high as they could go. He then grabbed the dope out of the red bag and placed a kilo on each burning eye of the stove. The flames began to grow more rapidly as the four kilos of dope began to disintegrate into the air.

"Man, what the fuck is you doin?!" Nate shouted in disbelief.

"I'm saving us from going to jail!" Nick snapped.

While Nick and Nate were still arguing, Tony Boy opened up the door with the chain still on it.

"Can I help y'all?" Tony Boy asked talking through the crack of the door.

The officer in the front charged into the door like a NFL linebacker, breaking the chain and knocking Tony Boy to the ground.

"Freeze motherfucker!" The officer yelled at Butch with his weapon drawn as Butch tried to run to the back of the house. "Butch Johnson, if you move I will blow the back of your brains out the front of your fucking face. Put your hands behind your head and get on the fucking ground!"

Nick and Nate were both terrified. When they had first come in, Nick pulled Nate with him in the basement that sat off the kitchen. They both stood on the basement landing awaiting their fate as they listened to the commotion on the other side of the door. Nate still had his weapon drawn and had every intention of using it.

The officer put the handcuffs on Butch and he didn't even attempt to resist. The truth was that he had been on the run for years and he was tired of running.

"Tony Boy, call my Mama and sister Sandy and tell her to come and bond me out. Tell 'em that this the last time. Tell 'em I promise I'm a change," Butch cried before he was thrown in the back of the squad car.

"Hey you!" The arresting officer yelled to Tony Boy. "You oughta clean your fucking house; it smells like shit in here. Oh, and sorry about the door."

All of the neighbors were on their porches watching what was going on and trying to ask Tony Boy questions, but he didn't pay them any mind. The moment the police rode off, he ran in the house to let the boys know that the coast was clear.

Tony Boy cracked the basement door. "C'mon, Bay Boy. They gone," He whispered like he was going to get in trouble if someone heard him.

Nate's black face turned burgundy as he looked at the $80,000 worth of ashes that coated the stove. At that very moment, Nick and Tony Boy were both more scared than they were when the police arrived. Not only was Nate an unpredictable fireball with a bad temper, but he had a loaded Uzi with two people to blame for his impromptu misfortune. So it was no telling what he might do next. In hopes of illuminating the dark situation, Nick decided to put his taciturn ways to the side and break the awkward silence.

"Look bro, Fred told me that the next time if we buy five bricks that he'd front us five more. I know that if I call him and tell him what happened—"

Before Nick could finish his sentence, he was rudely interrupted. "Man, fuck that bitch ass nigga Fred! Do you know what the fuck you just did?!" Nate yelled pointing the loaded Uzi in his face.

"Come on bro, chill out," Nick whispered in a merciful tone. He held both of his hands out in front of his face as if to block the barrage of bullets that could potentially come his way.

"Don't do it Bay Boy; just calm down," Tony Boy pleaded.

It was no doubt in both of their minds that Nate would blow their brains onto the kitchen floor, so it was a sigh of relief to them both when Nate lowered his weapon.

"You know what? I don't even know why I'm trippin'. We gone figure this shit out." Nate's sudden serene state of being was beginning to scare Nick and Tony Boy more now than when he first appeared to be upset.

"So Fred said that if we buy five, he'd front us five more, huh?" Nate asked, rubbing his chin as if he was enticed by the proposition.

"Yeah, but we have to give him $100,000 for the first five and then we'll have to owe him $100,000 for the other five," Nick explained. "But on the real, dude is a alright guy so if I tell him what happened, he'll probably work something out with us."

"Naw naw; fuck that! I got a even better plan and we ain't gone have to pay him shit."

"Bro, I hope you not talking about what I think you talking about."

"Yeah," Nate answered with malice in his voice. "That's exactly what the fuck I'm talkin' about."

Nick hoped that he was joking, but he knew that that was impossible with the look of death that was written on his face. Nate's face was so serious, cancer would look at him and smile.

"Fred and them would chop our fucking heads off if we tried some shit like that, and you know it," Nick pleaded.

"I know, and that's exactly why we going to kill him first," Nate stated firmly.

"Aw come on Bay Boy; y'all all grew up together. Y'all can't just kill Freddie…"

"Shut the fuck up!" Nate interrupted "It's yo' crackhead ass fault that this shit happened in the first place! If you woulda never had that nigga over here, none of this woulda never happened!" Nate looked like a bomb that was about to explode. Tony Boy may have just been high, but at one point, he could've sworn that he saw actual smoke coming from Nate's nose and ears.

Out of nowhere, Nate balled up his fist and hit Tony Boy with a haymaker right hook. You could hear the cartilage in his jaw shatter as the punch landed, dropping him to the floor. Tony Boy laid on the kitchen floor, curled up in a ball as Nate began to violently kick and stomp him anywhere he saw an opening. Nick stood in shock as he watched the beating. The flogging was beginning to be too much, so Nick decided to put an end to it. As Nick tried to grab Nate, he turned around throwing another vicious punch that once connected, knocked Nick to the ground. He then put the loaded Uzi up against his throbbing face.

"Touch me again and I'm a kill you," Nate warned. He then proceeded with the kicks and stomps until Tony Boy laid lifeless on the kitchen floor. Nate then grabbed a steak knife off the counter and violently stuck it into Tony Boy's abdomen three times. Nick thought that he was in a horror movie watching Tony Boy get beaten and stabbed like that. The puddle around his body was growing bigger and bigger as seconds went by. The steak knife that was still in Nate's hand had blood dripping off of it like a faucet that hadn't been completely turned off.

As Nick looked at him, he thought that he was staring at the Grim Reaper in the flesh. By the time Nate had realized what he had just done, it was too late. But he really didn't care because he wanted that type of fear embedded into Nick's head anyway. Nate came up with the plan to rob Fred, and Nick's involvement was essential. Without his participation, it would be impossible for him to get to Fred, so he had to make sure that he was on board.

"I had to kill him. We didn't have no choice," Nate began to justify. "If I didn't kill him, he would've told Fred and then we'd both be dead. You know you can't trust no motha fuckin' crack head. C'mon, dog and get up 'cause we got to get the fuck up outta here!"

Nate extended his hand to help Nick get up off the kitchen floor. After hesitating for a second, Nick took his hand and got up.

"So, what's next? What are we going to do now, bro?" Nick asked while rubbing his newly swollen jaw.

"Well, we know Tony Boy got his daddy back there all doped up, so he ain't waking up no time soon. We need to get this plan together, but first we gotta get the fuck up outta here." Nate peeked through the blinds to see if anyone was outside. "C'mon, let's go while ain't nobody outside. Get in your car and follow me to my crib," Nate ordered.

Nick nodded as he grabbed the bag that the drugs were in and headed for the door.

"Hold on right quick!" Nate shouted. He took the bloody steak knife out of his pants' pocket and knelt down to floor level. While looking at Nick with a nefarious look, he wiped the blood off the knife onto Tony Boy's shirt and left it on top of him.

"Now we can go." Nate said as they headed out the back door.

CHAPTER 6

It was pitch black by the time they made it to Nate's apartment. They came in through the patio door so that they didn't wake Shardae. Nate led Nick straight to the kitchen table so, they could discuss the plan. The plan was very simple, but he wanted Nick to feel comfortable. To ease the moment, he them poured them both small glasses of Hennessy. Nate twisted his face up, downed the first glass and poured himself another one.

"Listen dog, this is the simplest plan ever. Fred is having the party tomorrow and he thinks we're going to be in Ohio, right?"

"Right," Nick nodded as he took another sip from his glass.

"Okay, so we have Shardae and Cassandra take him up on his offer and go to his party. Now when the party is over, they gone leave with him. All of the money that he makes from the party is gone be on him."

"So what? We gone rob him for the party money?" Nick interrupted with a puzzled look on his face.

"Naw nigga; quit acting stupid!" Nate snapped. "The nigga gone be leaving the club high and drunk with two females and a bag full of money. So he's gone take them somewhere that he feels comfortable, like his house. And nine times out of 10, it's gone be some major dope and or money at that same location. So the girls gone have to do a little flirting, but they not gone do nothing with him. And as soon as the nigga falls asleep, they gone look around to see what they can find. And shit, if we get lucky enough, the nigga might just show them where everything is. Then the next day, we have the girls call him back and say that they had a good time and that they want to come back over. Now this is when he gone have his guard down and we'll be at his house waiting on him. Then we'll just kill him and take everything that he's got."

"But what if the girls don't find nothing? What if the house is empty?"

"Then we go to Plan B."

"What's Plan B?"

"If the girls don't find nothing on the first night, then we call him for the 10 bricks, kill him and take them."

Nick couldn't believe how Nate had masterminded two plans with such little preparation. The way that Nate talked about killing so insouciantly let Nick know that if he fucked up, he'd be a dead man. So he was a bit hesitant to bring up Tony Boy, but he had to. And he knew that Cassandra was going to freak out once she found out.

"So what about Tony Boy?" Nick asked before swallowing all of the spit in his mouth.

"What about him? I don't know nothing about no Tony Boy. I ain't seen him in two days."

"Bro, what am I gone tell San?"

"You ain't gone tell her shit 'cause you don't know shit. We'll find out when they find out. He probably owed a nigga some money for some dope and the nigga got tired of waiting," Nate suggested while shrugging his shoulders.

"So what about Butch?" Nick asked.

"Motha fuck Butch! You let me worry about Butch. Trust me, everything is gone work out just right. Now go home and tell Cassandra how Fred just sold us some fake dope, you feel me?" Nate said as winked an eye at Nick.

"Yeah, I got you bro."

"So go home and get some rest and make sure that y'all are back over here at 9:00 sharp so we can go over everything."

"Alright bro."

"9:00 sharp," Nate reiterated.

"Alright, I got you." Nick got in his car and sped into the night.

Shardae was awakened by the noise coming from the kitchen. She put her robe on over her panties and bra because she was unsure whether or not Nate had company. When she saw that it was just Nate, she let the front of the robe go, exposing her beautiful body. This was the perfect opportunity for her to make Nate want her and deny him the pleasure. He was going to pay for the way he acted at the restaurant. As she walked closer, she could tell that it was something wrong by the severity in his face.

"What's wrong?" Shardae asked, squinting because her eyes were still sensitive to the light.

"Sit down," Nate said as he took the last gulp of the Hennessy from his glass. "Fred sold us some fake dope today."

"What? Are you serious?!" Shardae asked in disbelief.

"Yup, he got us for 80 fucking thousand dollars!" Nate yelled as he slammed his fist on the table.

"Oh my God. So what now, I'm mean, what are we going to do?"

"Well, I got a plan that's gone get all our money back and some, but we gone need you and San to help."

"What do we have to do?"

"Look, we've got a long day ahead of us, so let's just go to bed and get some rest. Nick and Cassandra will be here in the morning, so we'll go over everything then."

Shardae complied and went to bed with him, but she couldn't help but wonder what was really going on and better yet, what was to come of this whole situation. She knew Nate too well and she was for certain that some blood was going to be shed behind this one.

Cassandra had been waiting on Nick to come home all night. She had called him several times, but he hadn't answered or returned any of her calls. Normally, she would make a big deal out of this, but she figured that he was probably still mad from earlier. In fact, she was starting to feel bad about what happened earlier. But tonight was going to be all about him. She had every intention of giving him the business as soon as he walked through the door. The strong smell of marijuana was starting to creep through the bathroom door, letting her know that Nick was home. She walked into the living room wearing nothing but the access water from the bath she had just taken. Something seemed odd because all of the lights were out and she knew Nick was there. She walked closer squinting into the darkness only to see Nick sitting at the kitchen table. She automatically knew that something was wrong.

"What's wrong baby?" Cassandra asked as she hit the light switch.

As the room lit up, she could see that one side of Nick's face was substantially larger than the other. He definitely had some explaining to do.

"What happened to your face?" Cassandra asked as she reached to grab his face to get a better look.

"Why don't you go and put on some fucking clothes!" Nick snapped as he snatched his face away from her hand.

Now she really knew that something was wrong. She went to grab her robe and rushed back to see what had happened.

"What happened, Nicholas?" She demanded while tying the front of her robe.

"Ain't shit happen. Me and Nate got into a little scuffle."

"Well, it don't look like no little scuffle. I shol' hope his face is fucked up, too."

"Listen, Fred sold us some fake dope and we started arguing and I punched him and he punched me back. He just hit me with a good one. It was two punches thrown and that was it."

"So let me get this straight. Fred sold y'all some fake dope and y'all started arguing, and you punched Nate and he punched you back?" Cassandra asked suspiciously with one eyebrow raised.

"Yeah, that's exactly what happened."

"Why would Fred sell y'all some fake dope?"

"I don't know, but we came up with a plan to get our money back, but you and Shardae gone have to help us."

"Okay, what's the plan?"

"Look baby, I'm tired as hell and we gotta be up to meet Nate and Shardae at 9:00 in the morning. So let's just go to sleep and we'll talk about it tomorrow when we get over there."

"Alright c'mon," Cassandra said as she reached for his hand.

Despite her wanting to really dig into his story, she complied and went to bed. For some reason, she knew that it was much more to the story than Nick was telling her. She didn't know exactly what it was, but she just had a gut feeling. One, she had known Fred for years and for him to sell someone some fake drugs was completely out of character. He had been hustling all of his life and he had never been known to do anything shady. And for two, Nick would never throw the first punch in a fight. The more she thought about Nick's story, the more she thought it was fishy. She knew that the truth would come out sooner or later, so she closed her eyes and tried to get some sleep, anxious to see what tomorrow would bring.

CHAPTER 7

Nick and Cassandra arrived at Nate and Shardae's apartment at 9:00 on the dot. Nate and Shardae were both drinking coffee at the kitchen table awaiting their arrival. They walked in the house and both had places set at the kitchen table. Nate had a blunt hanging from his lip that was stuffed with almost $50 worth of weed. He lit the blunt and got right down to business.

"Okay, look. So as y'all already know, me and my man Nick have a little problem and you two are the only people in the world that can help us right now," Nate began. "So let me just explain everything and when I'm done, I'll answer any question that y'all might have."

"Alright," both girls said in unison.

"So to make a long story short, Fred sold us some fake dope. I don't know what would possess him to do it, but he did it. Now I would just kill him, but me and

Nick would still be broke. And if we broke, then y'all broke. Now we came up with a plan that's very simple, but everybody has to play their role. Now he invited us to the party, so we want y'all to get real sexy and go," Nate continued. "He thinks me and Nick are gone be in Ohio, so after the party is over, we want y'all to leave with him and tell him that y'all want to go to his crib. You know, kinda flirt with him a little and tell him you want to see his house—whatever you have to say to get to his house. We need y'all to get him fucked up all while y'all in the club, so by the time you do get to his house, he gone be twisted and more than likely he's gone fall right to sleep. Soon as he falls asleep, we need y'all to find out what's there," Nate instructed. "The main thing we want is dope and money, but jewelry is cool, too. Now that's the first and most difficult part. The second part is easy as fuck. The following day, y'all gone call and tell him how much fun you had and that y'all are free for one more day and y'all want to go back out to his house. But you have to flirt a little to sell it. Now this time, when he picks y'all up, we'll be at the house waiting on y'all. It'll be like taking candy from a baby. Any questions?"

"What if this plan doesn't work?

"Trust me, San; it's gone work, baby. And when it's all over with, we gone give y'all $20,000 just for helping us."

"A piece?" Cassandra interrupted.

"Hell naw!" Nate said with his face twisted up. "Y'all get $10,000 a piece to do whatever the fuck you want to do. Any more questions?"

"No."

"So, do y'all think that y'all can handle it?"

They both nodded their heads yes. Since Cassandra was the more loquacious one of the two, she agreed to make the call. As she dialed the numbers on her cell phone, she thought that it was something fishy about this whole situation. But at this point she had to go with the flow because all of Nick and Nate's money was at jeopardy. Fred answered on the third ring.

"Hello."

"Hi, Fred," Cassandra said while putting the phone on speaker.

"Who is this?"

"Your favorite person in the world."

Right then, Fred knew exactly who it was. Your favorite person in the world had been Cassandra's signature saying since middle school.

"What's going on, San? Fred said, excited to hear her voice.

"Nigga, don't be tryin' to act like you know my voice."

"Once you said 'favorite person in the world,' you knew I was gone know who it was. So how are you, sweetheart?"

"I'm fine, how are you?"

"Shit, I'm laying across this $4,000 sofa in a pair of $50 draws smoking on a $150 blunt. I'm doing lovely."

"I can't stand you," Cassandra said, snickering.

Nate shook his head in disgust as Fred showboated over the phone. He couldn't wait to kill him.

"Where my girl Day Day at?"

"Hi Fred," Shardae answered as she moved closer to the phone.

"What's up Day Day; how you?"

"I'm fine."

"I asked you how you were doing and I didn't ask how you looked." Nate was becoming infuriated as he watched Shardae blushing on the phone. He was beginning to wonder if Shardae and Fred ever really did have a secret liaison. Coincidently, Nick was wondering the same thing about Cassandra.

"So y'all coming to the party tonight or are y'all chilling with the hubbies?" Fred asked, trying to find out if they had left for Ohio already.

"Naw, they're gone out of town for a few days," Cassandra answered, grabbing the phone back from Shardae. "That's why we called you. We want to make sure that if we come, you were going to show us a good time."

"Absolutely, I'm gone show y'all a excellent time. Don't worry about nothing. All y'all have to do is show up looking good, and I'ma take care of the rest. Drinks, weed, VIP—the whole nine yards. I got y'all. I'ma roll the red carpet out."

"Okay, well I guess we'll see you tonight. We'll call you when we get there."

"Okay bet. I'll see y'all tonight."

"Ok, we'll see you tonight, bye."

Everything was set. All the girls had to do was get sexy and go to the party. But first, they had another job to do. In order for the plan to work, Fred had to think that they were really out of town, so it was imperative that they stayed incognito. They sent the girls to get them enough alcohol, food, weed and cigarettes to last them for the rest of the day. Once the girls got them situated with everything they needed, they headed to Cassandra and Nick's apartment to get ready.

CHAPTER 8

Shardae and Cassandra had been getting prepped for the party for hours. Looking in the mirror at their "beauty pageant participant" resemblance let them know that all their hard work paid off. Cassandra had on a short white dress that was opened in a V-shape from her neck to her navel, exposing her heart shaped diamond studded belly ring. The back of the dress was open and the low cut exposed a small portion of her butt crack as she walked. The red high heels and red clutch offset the white dress and looked fierce with her red bob. Shardae was looking just as sexy. Her hair was in an effortless pony tail with her long black curls hanging out of the back of it. She was wearing an olive green and beige striped mini skirt with a beige sport coat that hugged her waist line. The fact that she wasn't wearing a bra or shirt underneath, forced her breasts to fight from protruding out of the jacket. She only had the middle button fastened allowing her belly ring and bursting cleavage to peak through. Her green and beige alligator peep toe high heels went perfectly with her ensemble. They both were guaranteed to be the sexiest women in the club. After calling Fred twice and not getting an answer, they still decided to head to the party.

Mouths dropped and heads turned as Cassandra and Shardae made their way toward the club entrance. They were both looking for Fred because the line to get in was wrapped around the corner and neither of them wanted to wait. Not to mention, both of them were looking far too good to be standing in line at some club. Before Cassandra could dial Fred's number a third time, she saw a familiar face signaling for her and Shardae to come to the front of the line. The familiar face was Diego. With the exception of his gold chain and teeth, he was dressed in all black as if he were about to commit a crime. Luckily for him, he wasn't because it would be far too facile to spot a dark complexioned criminal with a southern accent and a mouth full of gold.

"What's hattenin, shawty?" Diego greeted them with a smile so wide that they were able to count all 12 of his gold teeth. "Damn, y'all lookin gooder den a drop top Chevy!"

"Thank you," they both said in unison.

"C'mon, Fred got y'all a booth in VIP. He in hure waitin on y'all."

The girls followed Diego straight to the VIP section of the club. Luckily for them, they had VIP treatment because the club was shoulder-to-shoulder jam packed. Fred emerged from a crowd of people as the three of them walked up. The club lights were dancing off his jewelry like a disco ball. His two diamond link necklaces and Presidential Rolex watch made him look like he was glowing in the dark. Looking at the metal spikes that were coming out of his tennis shoes would put you under the impression that a porcupine had attacked his feet. He wore a striped Burberry T-shirt with the matching belt and a pair of ripped blue jeans shorts to match.

"What's up? How y'all doing?" Fred asked as he gave both of them a hug, spinning them around to check them out. "Got damn, y'all look good!"

Both girls blushed as he continued to shower them with compliments. He grabbed a hold of each of their hands and guided them to their VIP booth. Waiting on them at their booth was two champagne glasses and two bottles of Ace of Spade.

"Do y'all want something else to drink or is this cool?"

"Naw, this is cool."

"Yeah, this is fine," Shardae agreed.

"Not as fine as you are," Fred said, flirting with Shardae.

"But what about me?" Cassandra blurted out in a facetiously jealous way before Shardae could respond.

"Oh, you already know you fine, baby."

"Well, I need acknowledgement. If I got it, then tell me I got it then," Cassandra rapped in a sexy way with her hand on her hip.

"You definitely got it baby; both of y'all definitely got it."

They both blushed uncontrollably. Neither of them were used to this many compliments. Their boyfriends never told them how pretty they were, so they both wanted to savor the moment.

"Huunh, y'all want some Molly?" Fred offered as he pulled a small plastic bag out of his pocket.

"Yeah, give us some!" Cassandra said, excited to try it.

"Unt un, I'm not taking none of that," Shardae said prudishly.

"Girl, stop acting like that and take some with me."

"Naw. I don't even know what it does or how to do it."

"Girl, it makes you feel good," Cassandra said, trying to entice her.

"Day Day, I ain't gone never tell you nothing wrong, baby. All I ever want to do is make you feel good," Fred said, trying to entice her as well. "All you have to do is put a little in the champagne and drink it. You won't even know it's in there."

Shardae did not like taking any drugs, especially any new ones. Being the victim of peer pressure along with fact that she didn't want to ruin the vibe of the party, she gave in and allowed Fred to put some in the champagne. He poured them each a glass and began to drink as if it were regular champagne.

"We know it's Molly in here, so don't be trying to take us home and enjoy us," Cassandra said, flirting with Fred.

"Don't try to turn me on mentioning a good time," Fred flirted back with one eyebrow raised. "When are y'all boyfriends coming back?"

"In a few days," Cassandra said downing her glass of champagne.

"Well, I'ma be y'all boyfriends until they get back," Fred said being facetiously serious as he kissed them both on the cheek. A group of girls were signaling Fred to come over to their booth.

"Please excuse me for one second. I'll be right back."

The girls nodded and continued to drink. It had been almost 30 minutes since Fred had left and they were feeling the full effects of the Molly mixed with the champagne. Both of them were overwhelmed with joy. The exact feeling of the drug was indescribable. It was almost as if they had hit the Mega Millions and had an orgasm at the same time. The music in the club was beginning to sound better and better with each song. When Cal Commas' song *Whatever You Want* featuring Drey Skonie came on, they both started to dance on each other in such a provocative way that from the outside looking in, they looked like lesbians.

As Fred walked up, he stood in awe watching the two beautiful bodies grind up against one another. He blew clouds of weed smoke out of his mouth like an exhaust pipe while contemplating whether or not to go in for the kill. All night he had been flirting with them in a facetiously serious way. Just in case they turned him down or told their boyfriends, he would be able to blame it on the liquor and say that he was just playing. Fred decided to continue to play his little game and see where it would take him by the end of the night. He continued to watch them dance until the song went off and then took a seat in between them at the booth.

"Y'all having fun?" Fred asked knowing they were feeling the effects of the Molly by the way they danced.

"Yes. Oh my God! I feel so fucking good," Shardae replied.

"We're too fucked up to go home; we're coming with you," Cassandra whispered to Fred as she gently bit his ear.

"Y'all ready to leave now?" Fred asked smiling.

"Yeah," They both said in unison.

"Look, I'm finna let Diego know that I'm leaving, so just meet me in front of my Auntie Tracie's house on the South Side in 15 minutes."

The girls complied and left while Fred rushed to find Diego. He was out of breath by the time he finally found him.

"What's hattenin' main? Is you straight bruh?" Diego asked, reaching for his gun as if something was wrong.

"Yeah, yeah, I'm straight," Fred replied still trying to catch his breath. "But check this out. I'm 'bout to take Shardae and Cassandra out to the house, so I need you to wrap this shit up and grab all the money from the door."

"Main, is you sho' you wanna take them bitches out to the house, bruh?"

"Yeah dog, they straight."

"Alright bruh; I got cha."

The two of them slapped hands and Fred left to go and meet the girls. The whole idea of Cassandra and Shardae wanting to all of a sudden go home with Fred didn't sit too well with Diego, especially after the incident at the restaurant. He never thought it was a good idea to have women at the same place where you lay your head, period. But despite his warning, Fred said the girls were straight, so he just had to go with the flow and hope that no bullshit happens. 'Cause if it did, he'd be right there to solve any problem and murder was the only solution he knew.

CHAPTER 9

Cassandra and Shardae were parked in front of Fred's aunt's house patiently awaiting his arrival when a white sports car pulled up on the side of them.

"Come on; get in."

Fred was driving a white Ferrari Italia 458. Both Shardae and Cassandra were shocked as they saw the car. It looked like some sort of spaceship with the offset Rucci rims. They had never seen a Ferrari in real life; let alone rode in one. At that very moment, not only would they both have sex with Fred, but if they could, they'd copulate with the car. Shardae opened up the passenger side door and looked back at Cassandra with a puzzled look on her face. The car was only a two-seater.

"How are we supposed to fit in here?"

"Shit, y'all gone have to lap up," Fred replied, smiling as if this was all premeditated.

"Well, you gotta let me get in first, Day Day 'cause I ain't got no panties on."

"Bitch, you ain't never got no panties on," Shardae said jokingly as she slapped her on her butt.

"Day Day, it ain't no granny panties allowed in the Rari. So, if you got some on, you better leave them here."

"I wear thongs; thank you very much."

There wasn't a car in sight as Fred jumped on I-75. The freeway was emptier than the Secretary of State on a Sunday night. The car rode so smooth that it felt like he was doing 50 mph, although he was going well over 100 mph. The longer they sat, the better they were starting to feel. It was like the Molly had another level that was just now kicking in. They both began to get more comfortable kicking off their high heels. As Cassandra started to rub Shardae's thigh in a playful, yet sensual matter, Shardae swung her legs around, resting her pedicured toes on Fred's lap. She then turned to face Cassandra and they both started to kiss like they were taught in France. Cassandra's hand continued to trail up Shardae's skirt until she reached exactly where she was trying to go. As she crept her fingers into her panties, she felt nothing but the juices from her love box.

"Got damn, y'all can't wait till we get to the house? Y'all gone make me tear this car up," Fred said as he tried to drive and watch them at the same time.

With blatant disregard for Fred's wishes, Shardae took and stuck her foot up the right side of his shorts. He began to grow harder and harder and she continued to stroke her foot across him. In fact, he thought that if he got any harder that he might burst. Luckily, he was pulling up to his $500,000 condo.

With no hesitation or formal touring, he led them straight into the master bedroom. Shardae and Cassandra sat on the California king-sized bed and instantly began to kiss passionately. Cassandra unbuttoned Shardae's sport coat and sucked on her nipples like milk was about to come from them. She helped Shardae out of her skirt and panties and buried her head between her thighs. She began to moan uncontrollably as Cassandra gently scraped her teeth across her clitoris.

Fred had a beautiful view of Cassandra from behind. He walked up behind her and lifted up her dress in the back, exposing her Brazilian waxed goodies. As he stuck two of his fingers in her, feeling her warm, gushy insides, she turned around and grabbed him by his Burberry belt buckle, pulling him closer. She undid his shorts and pulled them to the floor along with his boxer briefs. She watched his tool pop out like a jack in the box. She began to slowly suck on it like it was her favorite Popsicle. His knees started to buckle as she twirled her tongue around the tip of his rod like a Ferris wheel. At that very moment, he had to stop her because he could no longer stand on his feet. He took off the rest of his clothes and laid across the bed completely naked with the exception of his jewelry and socks. As Cassandra sucked and caressed the head of his tool like it was the most precious thing in the world, Shardae joined in by tongue kissing his scrotum. Cassandra started to suck faster and faster while simultaneously stroking him. She could feel him pulsating in her mouth the faster she went. Then all of a sudden—Boom! Fluids shot out of him like a volcano. Cassandra and Shardae fought to ingest the fluids as if it were an antidote for eternal life. Shardae pushed Cassandra back onto the bed and dived her tongue between her legs. With her free hand, she began grabbing and tugging on Fred to get him back hard so she could guide him into her from behind.

"Oh my God!" Shardae cried out as she felt him sliding into her. "Oooh! Harder! Harder!"

Fred started pumping as fast as he could. The sound of his pelvis hitting her cheeks sounded like two hands clapping. His strokes became longer, slower and harder as he began to climax for the second time.

"Oh my God, Fred! Yas! Yas!" Shardae screamed as she began to climax.

Fred was exhausted. All of the drugs he took were starting to take a toll on his body. He laid back on the bed as if the ménage à trois was over.

"Naw, nigga. It ain't over with," Cassandra said with a confident smile.

She began to gently kiss on his soldier until it was back at full attention. Cassandra then bent Shardae over on all fours and explored her insides as if she was her gynecologist. She used her middle finger to search for her G-Spot while using her tongue to perform anilingus on her at the same time. Shardae began to climax almost instantaneously as Cassandra continued to stick her tongue in and out of her love tunnel while searching for her G-Spot.

"Oh my God! Please don't stop," Shardae begged as she began to climax for the second time, clinching the 1,000 thread count sheets.

"I'm ready now," Fred said, stroking himself before entering Cassandra from behind.

Cassandra reached behind and pulled him out of her. She took his piece and trailed it along her perineum until he was at the hole that she wanted him to enter. He opened up his mouth and let a glob of spit drip down her crack for lubrication to help him get inside. Cassandra grasp as he entered her threshold. As he started to pump vigorously, she tried to crawl away but couldn't because he had her by the waist.

"Oohh! Oohh!" Cassandra screamed.

She tried to put her hand back there to slow him down, but it was no stopping him. He continued to pump until he exploded for the third time. And by that time, Cassandra had exploded twice herself. Her legs began to quiver as she tried to stand.

"Where's the bathroom?" Cassandra asked.

"Right there," Fred pointed, completely out of breath.

Still completely nude, Shardae and Cassandra both walked into the master bathroom.

"Girl, I feel like we were both just in a porno movie," Shardae whispered as she sat on the toilet.

"Me too, but don't forget what we came here to do," Cassandra whispered as Shardae got off the toilet and she sat down to take her turn. "As soon as he passes out, I'm a look around and see what I can find. You just stay in the bed with him in case he wakes back up. Then you can put his ass back to sleep."

After a quick wash up, they walked back in the bedroom and to their surprise, Fred was sound asleep. He had somehow managed to take off his jewelry and put on his boxer briefs before passing out. Shardae put on her panties and one of his T-shirts that was folded on the dresser and laid in bed beside him, praying that he wouldn't wake up. In the meantime, and still completely nude, Cassandra proceeded to ransack the house.

It was almost 4:30 in the morning, and Nick and Nate were still up. With the exception of the television, the apartment was completely silent and dark. Empty potato chip bags and pop cans were scattered across the coffee table. The loose tobacco fillings from numerous cigars filled the empty Domino's pizza box that sat on the floor. Despite the two of them chain smoking and drinking all night, neither of them could fall asleep. But Nate wasn't trying to fall asleep; in fact, he wasn't even watching TV. Shardae and Cassandra were clearly staying the night with Fred, but he wanted to wait up just in case. Nate was very jealous and insecure, and he didn't completely trust Shardae. Just the thought of what she could potentially be doing had him livid. Nate sat there in deep thought. The cigarette in between his fingers that he'd lit two minutes ago continued to burn in its indolent state, making its ashes longer than the actual cigarette. As he glanced over at Nick, he envisioned himself strangling him until his eyes popped out.

"You straight bro?" Nick asked, breaking the reverie.

"Yeah," Nate answered as he walked into the kitchen to fix another drink.

Right now, Nate had great feelings of aversion towards Nick. In his eyes, the whole situation was Nick's fault. If he would've never had Butch over to

Tony Boy's house, none of this would've never happened. He never even understood why Butch was there in the first place. But in all actuality, greed is what put them into this predicament and greed was the only thing that was keeping Nick alive. Nick played an essential role in this plan and that was the only reason why Nate hadn't killed him yet. As soon as they got what they were going to get from Fred, Nick could die. Nate just needed a justifiable reason and he had every intention on finding one, even if he had to create one.

CHAPTER 10

Cassandra started her search in the walk-in closet that was attached to the master bedroom. Walking in the closet made her in awe of the shopping mall emulation. He had at least 100 pairs of shoes and every other high-end item from Persian lamb jackets to full length mink coats. He clearly had great fashion sense. She rumbled through a few drawers. Other than a few small trinkets, she found nothing.

As she tiptoed through the living room, she was shocked by the first thing that she noticed. She had never seen anything like this before in her life. The focal point of the room was a pool table that sat on a platform doubling as a fish tank. Looking at the pool table reminded her of when her and Nick took a trip to Puerto Rico last summer and swam in the Caribbean Sea. The multitude of exotic fish made the pool glow in the dark. She continued to rummage, making her way to the first bedroom.

The squeaking sound of the door made her whole body tense up as she tried to quietly push it open. She got the door open just enough to squeeze through and realized that the room was completely empty. The closet was even empty. There was another room that sat cater-corner to the room she was just in. As she went to twist the knob, something was impeding her entrance. The door was locked. That alone let her know that it was something in the room worthy of the door being locked. She grabbed a bobby pin out of her hair and went to work. Years ago, her uncle taught her how to pick a lock and she never understood why because she thought that she would never have to. The teaching came in handy because the door was open in less than a minute.

Immediately upon entrance, she noticed how modest the room was compared to the rest of the house. The only thing visible was a queen-sized bed and a dresser. There was no reason for the door to be locked on a room so modest unless there was something major being hid inside of it. She quietly opened the top two drawers on the dresser. They both were filled with rubber bands. Her street senses tingled instantly. There were only two reasons for a person to have this many rubber bands—they were going to be braiding a lot of hair, or counting a lot of money. And Fred didn't look like the type to braid hair.

She opened the closet door and was shocked at the arsenal of weapons. There were two AK-47s, two Uzis, a shotgun and four pistols which, with the exception of the shotgun, all had extended clips.

She closed the closet door and got on her hands and knees to take a look under the bed.

It was hard for her to make out what she was seeing through the darkness, but it looked like some type of luggage. As she pulled one of the bags from under the bed, she could see that it wasn't just any luggage; it was a Louis Vuitton duffle bag. Her brown eyes turned green as she unzipped the duffle bag. The bag was full of money and there were two more bags under the bag. She quickly zipped the bag and placed it back exactly where she had got it from so no one would notice that it had been moved.

Seeing all of that money made her sober all the way up as if she hadn't been doing drugs and drinking all night. Her mind began to race as she thought about all the things that her and Nick could do with all of that money. Now she knew for a fact that a Neiman Marcus shopping spree was imminent. She closed the door and rushed back to the master bedroom trying not to make a sound. To her surprise, Fred and Shardae were both sleep. She put on a T-shirt that was folded up on the dresser, got in bed next to Fred and went to sleep.

CHAPTER 11

It was 7:30 in the morning and it was a frenzy going on inside the police department. People were slapping and celebrating like their favorite baseball team had just won the World Series. Maybe it was because Detective Sanchez just made the biggest marijuana bust in the city's history, or maybe it was because Captain McGraw had decided not to retire after all. Either way, the department was in pure tumult until Captain McGraw brought all of the commotion to an abrupt end.

"Sanchez, I need to see you in my office."

"Alright, Cap," Detective Sanchez replied as he continued to fumble around in his desk.

"Right now, got dammit!" Captain McGraw shouted irately.

Noticing the severity of the request, Detective Sanchez got right up and followed him into his office.

Captain McGraw had been on the force for over 30 years and was almost forced to retire after rumors of his malfeasance began to spread. But when the person with all of the alleged information turned up dead in a gun deal gone bad, he decided not to retire and came back to work like nothing ever happened. To be such a small man, he was quite a formidable figure on the task force. He was a pudgy white man in his mid–fifties, whose balding hair made him look like the before picture for a Hair Club for Men commercial.

Detective Sanchez, on the other hand, was in his mid-twenties and had a very slim built. He was up and coming with something to prove. He felt inferior as he sat in the little chair that looked up to the throne of a chair that seated Captain McGraw.

"Here's the deal, Sanchez. Two days ago on the South Side, somebody tried to kill a crackhead by the name of Antonio Brown aka Tony Boy. Now, we had an anonymous caller tip us off that Butch Johnson was hiding out at Tony Boy's house the same day that he was almost killed. So apparently, somebody tried to kill him some time after a unit went in his house and arrested Butch." Captain McGraw slid the files across his desk to

Sanchez. "Butch is still in the county jail, and Tony Boy is still screwed up in the hospital. I don't know what the fuck is going on, but you're sure in the hell going to find out 'cause I'm putting you on the case."

Detective Sanchez was ecstatic. He had been begging to get put on a big case for months, and now he was finally getting the opportunity. Sanchez wondered how he had gotten so lucky with the case, but it was clearly a sign of nepotism, seeing as how he was the step-nephew of Captain McGraw. Plus, he had just stumbled across the biggest marijuana bust in the city's history, so he felt like he deserved to be on the case.

"Thank you so much, Captain."

"Shut up and listen and you listen good, got dammit. Do not fuck this up. Do you understand me?"

"Yes sir, Captain. Yes sir."

"Alright, now get the fuck outta my office. And quit with all the 'yes sir' bullshit. You make me feel old."

Fred awoke to two, beautiful half-naked women in bed with him. For an average, this would be a dream come true; but for Fred, this was just another typical morning. He reeked from the smell of unprotected sex and still felt sluggish from all the drugs he took the night before. The shower was calling his name, so after putting on a pot of coffee, he got right in and tried to wash the excess DNA off his body. For the most part, last night was a blur. He had a vague recollection of the event that took place. What he did remember is that he was very inebriated, he had an awesome threesome with Shardae and Cassandra, and he didn't wear any condoms. So now other than their boyfriends, he had two more things to worry about: a possible sexually transmitted disease, and/or a potential pregnancy.

He was really starting to feel Shardae. It was something about her that he just couldn't put his hands on. Cassandra was cool and she was awesome in bed, but it was just something different about Shardae. In fact, he liked her so much that if she would sanction it, he would have Nate killed just so they could be together. As he got out of the shower and grabbed his coffee, he could see that the girls were still sleeping. He sat down on the bed next to Shardae and began to gently rub his fingers through her curly black hair until she woke up.

"Good morning, sexy," Fred whispered, trying not to wake Cassandra up.

"Good morning. What time is it?" Shardae asked as she sat up rubbing her eyes.

"It's 8:13."

"Dang, it's still early."

"They say a sleeper don't get nothing but dreams. It's some brand-new toothbrushes on the bathroom sink. So, how about you go and brush your teeth 'cause your breath stank and meet me on the patio," Fred said jokingly as he frowned, turning up his lip like the smell of her breath was unbearable.

"Shut up," Shardae said as she got up and headed to the bathroom.

It was a beautiful morning outside. The view of the sun's rays beaming off the river looked like something you would only see on a postcard. Fred sat on the loveseat and sipped his coffee while enjoying the awesome view. Shardae came right out and sat on his lap, wearing the same thing that she went to sleep in last night. She leaned in and placed a slow, passionate kiss onto his lips.

"Does my breath smell better now?" Shardae asked sarcastically.

"Much better," Fred said smiling. "You want a cup of coffee?"

"No thanks." As Shardae stared into the river, she fell into deep thought. She was starting to feel extremely guilty. The same man she felt herself falling for was about to be robbed and murdered by her boyfriend and she was helping to make it all possible.

"Day Day," Fred said breaking her reverie, "I think you should leave your boyfriend and be mine full time."

A plethora of mixed feelings began to flow through her body. She was so shocked by the statement that she slid off his lap and sat in the seat next to him.

"Fred, you know I can't just leave Nate. He would literally kill me," Shardae said in a serious voice.

"He won't do nothing to you if you're my girl. I'll always keep you safe."

"I just can't, Fred. I can't."

They both got quiet as Cassandra walked in wearing Fred's T-shirt with one of the bedsheets wrapped around her.

"I'm jealous. Ain't nobody invite me to the party," Cassandra said sarcastically as she sat on Fred's lap.

"Shid. We wasn't doing nothin' but sittin' out here and enjoyin' this view. You were sleeping so peacefully that I didn't wanna wake you up," Fred said while rubbing her back, trying not to make her feel left out. "It's some brand new tooth brushes in the—"

"Oh, I already got one," Cassandra said cutting him off. "I saw it sitting on the vanity when I got up and I figured it was for me."

"You want some coffee?"

"Naw, I'm okay," Cassandra said as she stretched her legs onto Shardae's lap to get more comfortable.

Shardae was still in deep thought about the enticing offer Fred had just made. Her thought process was suddenly overcome by a bit of jealousy as she watched Fred insouciantly play in Cassandra's hair.

Cassandra wasn't wearing any panties and she could feel Fred getting hard through his robe as she moved her big round bottom around on him. She then discreetly stuck her hand under his robe and began to play with him. Despite her best endeavor to conceal what she was doing, Shardae knew exactly what was going on and decided to put an end to it.

"San, don't you think we need to get going?"

"Yeah, you're right. We do need to get going."

Cassandra stood up and headed in while Shardae and Fred followed close behind. Fred was hesitant for a second because he wanted to allow all of his blood to return to the areas where it normally resided. On the way in, Shardae turned and grabbed him by his still semi-erect tool.

"You're not ready to have a girlfriend," Shardae whispered in a jealous tone.

Fred just smiled and shrugged with the "what did I do?" look on his face. They all got dressed and Fred dropped them back off at their car which was still parked in front of his Auntie's house.

"So, when are we going to hang out again?" He asked as he pulled up behind Shardae's car.

"They should be back tomorrow, so we can probably hang out later on tonight," Cassandra answered.

"That's cool with me. Just call me a little later and let me know what time."

"Alright, we'll call you later on," Shardae said as they carefully got out of the big dually truck.

They now had to rush to Cassandra's apartment to take showers and change clothes before going back to Shardae's house to meet up with their boyfriends. They had such a great time last night, but now it was time for them to snap back into reality because they had big business to tend to.

CHAPTER 12

Butch sat in the interrogation room puzzled. He didn't have the slightest idea as to what exactly was going on. All he knew was that he was called out of his holding cell because the detective wanted to talk to him. His mind began to race about all of the crimes he had recently committed and gotten away with. Maybe it was the prostitute he body-slammed and robbed after being dissatisfied with her oral services. Or maybe it was the lawn mower he got caught stealing after the owner's dog attacked him. Or maybe it was some kind of mistake. He hoped that it was just some kind of mix-up because with his list of charges and criminal history file as thick as the Yellow Pages, the judge would be sure not to show him any leniency. Detective Sanchez walked in and got straight down to business.

"So what happened at Tony Boy's house?"

"Man, how you gone ask me all these questions and not even give me a square? I need a square or a brew or something."

"You'll get your cigarette as soon as you tell me what happened at Tony Boy's house."

"What you mean what happened at Tony Boy's house?" Butch asked, not knowing what was going on.

"The day you got arrested from Tony Boy's house, I need to know exactly who was there and what was going on."

"Well, I'll tell you everything you wanna know, but I need to be cut loose wit all charges dropped. And I need $275 in all cash."

"This is how it works, Butch. The more information you tell me, the more I can do for you. So what cha got?"

"Okay, it was me, Tony Boy, Nick and Nate."

"Who is Nick and Nate, and what is their last names?"

"I think they Tony Boy's little cousins or something, and I don't know no last names."

"Well, what do they look like?"

"Well Nate is a lil' black, cocky, ugly "Whoopi Goldberg" lookin' nigga wit long dreadlocks. And Nick is a lil' tall, light-skinned "Prince" lookin' mothafucka."

"So what were you guys doing?" Detective Sanchez asked as he began to write in his small notepad.

"Well, me and my main man Tony Boy was 'bout to get high and he smoked up all my damn dope, so I kicked his ass."

"You kicked his ass?" Detective Sanchez asked with one eyebrow raised.

"Hell yeah!" Butch confirmed. "I swung on him and knocked him out, then he got up and tried to kick me but I choke slammed him and—"

"Get to the point! What were Nick and Nate doing?" Detective demanded, sensing the mendacity in Butch's story.

"Tony Boy went to the store and when he came back, he said the police was outside. And Nick had a whole bunch of kilos in a bag—"

"Kilos of what?" Detective Sanchez interrupted.

"Dope! The kilos was full of crack cocaine and hair-ron," Butch continued. "So Nick got scared and put four of the keys on the stove and burned 'em up."

"And then what?" Detective asked, waiting for the rest of the story.

"That's it. They kicked in the door and took my black ass to jail."

"Alright, thank for your time sir," Detective said as he closed his notepad and put it in the back pocket of his khaki pants, heading for the door.

"Hold on man! Hold on! What happened to the square?" Butch asked, reminding him of the cigarette he had promised.

"I'm sorry, I forgot. I don't even smoke," Detective Sanchez said as he walked out of the door.

"You bitch made mothafucka!" Butch yelled.

Detective paid the comment no attention. He had gotten all of the information that he needed. Now it was time for him to make his way to the hospital and pay Tony Boy a visit.

As Fred pulled off, he received a call from Diego. He had forgotten all about having him wrap things up at the club last night. He had projected to make at least $20,000 off the party and he knew that Diego was trying to bring him the money. Plus, he knew that Diego wanted a full rundown of what happened with Cassandra and Shardae.

"Hello?" Fred answered on the second ring.

"Wuz up main; where ya at?"

"I just dropped off ole girl and dem."

"You just droppin' dem hoes off, bruh?"

"I just dropped them off about two minutes ago. But I got to tell you about last night. Dog, I freaked wit' them all night," Fred stated boastfully.

"Main, both of 'em?"

"Both of 'em," Fred replied.

"Oooh weee! When you goin' back to da crib, main? I know you got dat shit on tape bruh."

"You already know it's on tape, dog. But where you at cause I'm on my way to the crib now."

"Ok, I just dropped my gurl off at work. I'm on my way right nah."

"Alright bye."

One thing about Fred was that he dealt with a lot of people, so he had a lot of trust issues. He had spy cameras installed in every room of every house that he had ever owned. That way, if something ever came up missing, he'd know exactly who took it, plus it gave him endless freak hours of freak footage. Little did he know that by looking at the tapes, he'd be getting a lot more than he bargained for.

"Bitch, we 'bout to be rich!" Cassandra yelled as she got in Shardae's car.

"Girl what did you find?"

"I found four Louie bags full of money!"

"Where at?" Shardae asked.

"In one of the bedrooms underneath the bed."

"How much money do you think was in it?"

"I don't know Day Day, but it was a whole lot. It might've been like a million dollars."

"A million dollars?!" Shardae asked as her eyes got big and her face lit up.

A million dollars was a lot of money and at that very moment, she knew that Fred was a dead man. Nate was a very greedy man and she knew that for a million dollars, he'd probably kill her, so killing Fred would be a piece of cake and it was nothing that she or Cassandra could do about it. At this point, they were both in too deep, so their only option was to just go with the flow. Right now they had to hurry to Cassandra's house so they could shower and change before going back to Shardae's house with their men. Both girls knew that they would be attacked with an interrogation upon their arrival, but luckily the information that they had was so valuable that the guys would probably forget to even ask about all of the details.

CHAPTER 13

Fred arrived at the condo first, so he decided to take a shower before Diego got there. After the shower, he threw on a gray Polo jogging suit, a pair of Air Jordans and awaited Diego's arrival. To his surprise, Diego had already let himself in and was watching the surveillance tape on the 90-inch plasma television that was mounted on the wall.

"Main, you a fool fa dis one!" Diego said laughing.

"Dog, both of them hoes are some diabolical freaks!" Fred said boastfully as he pointed to the TV screen.

"Got damn, main!" Diego yelled, grabbing his crotch as he continued to watch the porn movie of a surveillance tape.

"Is that the money from the party?"

"Yeah main! You $21,000 richer," Diego replied as he threw Fred the brown paper bag full of money.

Fred emptied the contents of the bag on the pool table and proceeded to count it. It wasn't that he didn't trust Diego because they were like brothers; he simply just wanted to double check. He knew that Diego liked to use money counters and Fred hated them. His philosophy about money counters was that they were manmade machines that were subject to malfunction. He, on the other hand, had been counting money for years and would never malfunction. He continued counting as Diego watched the tape in awe, wishing he had been a part of it.

"Main, dem hoes put you to sleep like a baby!" Diego yelled referring to how fast Fred fell asleep.

As the girls came out of the bathroom, Diego watched Cassandra tiptoe into the closet. He really didn't think too much of it until he saw how uneasy Shardae was looking. Then it registered in his brain—why would she be in the closet in the first place? Diego pressed the button on the remote to split the screen, enabling him to see the surveillance of all the cameras at the same time. Fred getting this system installed was ingenious. This had to have been the best $10,000 that he has ever spent because it was like watching reality television. Diego watched carefully as Cassandra picked the lock on the door of the money room and began rifling through the closet and drawers.

"Dog, you know them hoes supposed to call me back to….What the fuck is this?!"

Fred yelled as he interrupted his own self looking at the TV screen. "Them dirty dust mop bitches!" Fred yelled punching his hand with his fist.

"I bet it was Nate who put 'em up to it, main," Diego suggested.

"Yeah, but Nick was in it, too. That's why both of them hoes came."

"So, what you wanna do, main?" Diego asked, ready for whatever.

"Just hold tight, dog. They found all the money and didn't take it. That means they gone try to come back to get it and when they do, we gone be waitin' on 'em," Fred said shrewdly with one eyebrow raised.

To Fred, life was a big game of chess. Not only did he always plan and think five moves ahead, but he always thought about his opponents' next moves so he could counterattack. Now that he knew their next move, he could set it up so they could walk right into his death trap. Now they had to play the waiting game and wait on the girls to call so they could counter-attack, but little did Fred know he was about to receive an unexpected phone call that would make his plan that much easier.

Nick and Nate were both knocked out on the sofa when the girls came in. Luckily, they weren't there to kill them because if they were, then they'd be dead. The place was a mess; it stunk of smoke and old food. It would make you think that some teenagers lived there without any adult supervision. The 10 or so cocktails that sat in the ashtray let the girls know that they had chain smoked themselves to sleep.

"Hellooo!" Cassandra shouted enough for the whole neighborhood to hear her.

Both Nick and Nate jumped as they were suddenly awaken. They were both happy to see that their girls had finally made it and were anxious to find out what had happened.

"Damn, you scared the shit out of me," Nick said, rubbing the crust out of his eyes.

"So what happened? What did y'all find?" Nate asked, getting straight to the point.

"Well, after the party, Fred took us back to his place—"

"Where at?" Nate interrupted.

"Damn, can I finish?" Cassandra asked, looking at Nate with both of her hands on her hips.

"My fault. Go ahead, I'm all ears."

"Thanks you," Cassandra said sarcastically. "The condo is downtown, off the river at the Water Gate. After we went to his house, we had a few drinks and he passed out. I started looking around and in one of the rooms, it was a bunch of guns in the closet and under the bed was four bags full of money."

"How much money was in each bag?" Nate interrupted.

"I don't know, but it was four of them and they were all filled up to the top."

"Was the money loose or was it in rubber bands?" Nick asked.

"It was in all rubber bands."

"Are you sure they were all filled with money?" Nate asked.

"I'm positive that one was filled up with all money, but I didn't check the other ones 'cause I was scared and I thought I had heard a noise, but they have to be money. What else could they be?"

"Dope," Nick said. "The other three bags could have been full of bricks."

"How many stacks do you think was in the bag?" Nate asked.

"I don't know, but it was a whole bunch."

"Listen, Cassandra," Nate said slowly. "I need for you to remember how many stacks were in the bag."

"I don't know! It was dark and I wasn't trying to get caught. But they looked just like the stacks that we count for y'all and it was probably about two or 300 of 'em in the bag."

"It had to have been all money! Niggas always keep money and dope in separate spots. And if it's as much as she says, then that's like a million dollars! We got to have all of that!" Nate shouted.

The M word made everyone's eyes light up green. There was suddenly a plethora of greed in the air. The room became so silent that you could hear spiders having sex. Everyone was thinking of all the possibilities.

"So listen y'all; this is the plan. Y'all gone have to call him a little later and say that y'all want to chill with him again. After that, all y'all have to do is get him to pick y'all up and go back to his crib. Me and Nick'll take it from there. Now does anybody have any questions?"

"Yeah. Let me ask you this bro. Just 'cause the money was there last night doesn't mean that it'll still be there tonight, right?" Nick asked, making a valid point.

"That's a good question," Nate answered. "But lemme tell you why. Evidently that's his safe house. If he was gone move that money, then it wouldn't have even been there in the first place. He's got that money in a place that's he feels is safe. Trust me that money has been there for a few days and it'll be there for a few more."

"You right bro, you right," Nick nodded in agreement.

"So what time do you think we should call him?" Shardae asked.

"Aw, we gone wait till about eight when it starts getting dark. Plus it's supposed to rain later. Are there any more questions?"

Everyone shook their heads saying no. So far, Nate's plan was going better than he thought. In fact, he thought that his deficient plan would be his demise, but suddenly things were starting to look up. Nick's only dilemma now was to leave Nate's house with Cassandra so that he could give her a fabricated version of his plan. If he couldn't leave that house, his plan would be completely ruined; so it was imperative that he and Cassandra leave. With all that was going on, Nick knew that leaving would be easier said than done. He knew that Nate wasn't just about to let them go with an estimated million dollars at stake. At this point, time was of the essence and Nick was beginning to over think the whole situation. So instead of making up some bullshit excuse, he decided to give Nate the most feasible reason for him and Cassandra to leave. Nick took in a big gulp of air and swallowed.

"Aye bro, me and San are going to go and chill at the crib for a minute. We got a long night ahead of us and I want to get some rest before we take care of this tonight."

Despite Nick being a taciturn coward, at the end of the day, he and Nate were supposed to be like brothers. He knew that Nate had enough respect not to snap and embarrass him in front of his girl. And that's exactly why he made sure that the girls were right there.

"Man, you know that we can't let nobody see us nowhere. Nigga, it's a million dollars at stake! And if somebody sees us, it's over. We can't risk that!"

"Yeah, you right bro, but I got my dope fiend car and the windows are tinted. Plus, I need to relax alone with my girl so I can get my mind ready for tonight."

"Alright, but lemme holler at you in the kitchen for a second before y'all leave," Nate said in a mellow voice.

Nick led the way to the kitchen and as soon as he turned around, he thought he was face to face with Satan. If looks could kill, he'd be DOA. With this much money at stake, the average person would cross their own mother.

"Look dog, don't try no bullshit and make me kill you," Nate warned Nick.

Nick stood there with an appalled, yet puzzled look on his face as if he were really hurt by the comment. "I can't even believe you would say that, bro. I would never do nothin—"

Nate interrupted in mid-sentence. "Look dog, just go home and take care of your business. But make sure y'all are back here at 7 o'clock on the dot."

"Alright bro," Nick said and got Cassandra and they headed out the door.

CHAPTER 14

Cassandra's clairvoyance kicked in at rapid speed. She knew that something was wrong when Nate pulled Nick into the kitchen. Four million dollars was a lot of money, and she knew exactly what greed would do to someone in the time of need. Thinking about all of the factors involved made her worry about her and Nick's safety. One thing that she was taught at an early age was that in a kill or be killed situation, you always kill. That was how her parents both got killed and she wasn't going out like that. She had to see where Nick's head was at.

"Why did Nate want to talk to you in the kitchen?"

Nick wasn't paying her any attention. He was too busy driving and thinking of a smooth way to fabricate his plan to her because he knew that it was impossible for him to put all of his cards on the table. "What?" Nick asked in an irritated voice upon recognizing that Cassandra had asked him a question.

"I said, why did Nate wanna talk to you in the kitchen?"

"Aw, that wasn't nothing. He was just telling me some shit about last night," Nick lied.

"So if he was just telling you something about last night, then why were you looking like that?"

"Lookin' like what?"

"Nigga, I saw the look on your face when he was talking to you and you looked like a scared puppy."

"I wasn't looking like no mothafuckin' scared puppy!" Nick yelled showing that he was offended and embarrassed by her comment.

"You know what, Nick? You better have a mothafuckin' plan. 'Cause four million dollars is a lot of mothafuckin' money and you know how greedy Nate is. Something could easily happen to us and all of that money would be his. But if something were to accidentally happen to him, we could still give Day Day his half," Cassandra suggested with one eyebrow raised.

"Girl, what the hell are you talking about?" Nick asked, knowing exactly what she was talking about.

"You know exactly what I'm talking about. If something were to happen to him, then we wouldn't have to worry about anything happening to us."

"C'mon, let's go," Nick said tapping her thigh as he pulled into the apartment complex. "I already got a plan. I'm 'bout to call Fred."

Tony Boy had finally regained consciousness after his surgery. As he opened his eyes, he found himself in a sudden state of bewilderment. He didn't know where he was at or what was going on. Clearly, he was in the hospital, hence the IV in his arm; but he didn't have a clue as to how he had gotten there or what exactly had happened to him. All he knew was that he was in excruciating pain. It felt like his stomach was being held together by barbed wire, so he must've just gotten stitches. All of a sudden, Tony Boy forgot about his pain as the most beautiful white woman he had ever seen entered the room. She had the body of a video vixen; the way that the powder blue scrubs fit her would make you think that they were a whole size too small. She wore her long blonde hair in a pony tail that swung back and forth as she walked. Tony Boy was speechless as he stared into her big brown eyes.

"Hi, I'm Capri," the nurse introduced herself.

"And I'm very pleased to meet you, Bay Girl," Tony Boy responded in a smooth voice.

Despite being stabbed and beaten, Tony Boy's suavity didn't go anywhere. Over the years, his good looks may have deteriorated, but his womanizing ways had yet to vanish. He was beginning to feel young again and the more he looked at Capri, the more he became in awe of her beauty. In fact, he was so mesmerized that he forgot to even ask her what happened to him.

"Well, Mr. Brown—"

"Please, call me Tony," he interrupted.

"Well, Tony, your surgery went very well. Your spleen was successful removed and you're looking at a full recovery in six to eight weeks. I'll be coming to check on you periodically throughout the day, but you can press the button on your right and it'll page me at the front desk. The button to your left is morphine and it will only release a dose of the medicine every 30 minutes, so try to use it sparingly. And if you get hungry, you can call down to the kitchen and order anything off the menu. Do you have any questions?"

"Yeah, uh, is there any way I could get a sponge bath?" Tony Boy asked, smiling.

"Absolutely, I'll have John come in right away."

"Whoa, whoa who the hell is John?"

"John is the CNA, whose responsibility it is to give you a sponge bath," Capri replied.

"Naw, naw. I'm straight, Bay Girl. I can take a bird bath or something."

Before Capri could respond, a slim Caucasian man dressed like a substitute teacher walked in. He had on a pair of loose khaki pants with a cheap plaid shirt that could've doubled as a tablecloth.

"Hi, I'm Detective Sanchez. I need to speak with Mr. Brown for a moment."

"Sure," Capri responded before walking out of the room.

"Hi Mr. Brown. I'm Detective Sanchez. How are you feeling?"

"I feel like shit. It feels like I just had a C-Section."

"Well, that's why I'm here, sir. I need to ask you a few questions so that we can get to the bottom of what happened and find the people who did this to you."

"How about you tell me what the hell happened?! I don't know what the fuck is going on!" Tony Boy yelled belligerently.

"Well, Mr. Brown, you were beaten up pretty badly and stabbed several times with a steak knife. In fact, you are very lucky to be alive. Your next-door neighbor heard some loud commotion and when she came over to see what was going on, she found you in a puddle of blood. The only other person in the house was your father and your same neighbor has been staying there with him since the incident. We're still trying to figure out the motive because there was no sign of forced entry and nothing was missing from the house…"

"Hold on Bay Boy! It's all kinds of shit missing," Tony Boy interrupted.

"But sir, your father and neighbor said that everything was there."

"Naw, naw, I'm talking 'bout the shit I had on me. Somebody took my shit out of this room."

"What exactly did you have, sir?"

"I had $278 in cash money in my pocket, a bridge card that I hadn't even used yet, a pair of brand-new Steph Curry's gym shoes, and I had one of them $1,500 belts, too."

"So you had $278 in cash, a bridge card, a pair of Steph Curry gym shoes, and a $1,500 belt?" Detective Sanchez said as he began jotting in a small notepad. "And exactly what kind of belt cost $1,500?" Detective Sanchez asked sarcastically.

"It was one of them uh, a Hep, awh a Herm, a Herpez, yeah a Herpez. My niece got it for me for Christmas."

"Okay Mr. Brown, let me ask you this. You were in a coma for 48 hours, so how do you remember all of this?" Detective Sanchez asked suspiciously.

"So what you trying to say, Jack? I'm lying?"

"Well, for one, sir, my name isn't Jack; it's Detective Sanchez. And for two, I really don't give a flying fuck about a Herpes belt or a bridge card!" Detective Sanchez snapped, now losing his patience. "All I want to know is what you remember about the incident that took place at your house two days ago!"

"Well, dig dis here, Jack. I was in a coma, ya dig, so I don't remember shit."

"What can you tell me about Butch Johnson?"

"I don't know no nigga name Butch."

"What about Nate and Nick?" Detective Sanchez asked as he read the names off his notepad.

"I don't know them niggas neither."

"Oh really? That's interesting because Butch Johnson was arrested from your house prior to the incident. Nick and Nate were there with you guys, also. We received an anonymous tip saying that a fugitive by the name of Butch Johnson was being harbored at your home. Phone records show that the call was made from the Pope residence about 30 minutes prior to the incident. And coincidently, the Popes stay one block over from you. Now, are you sure that you don't know Butch, Nick or Nate?"

"Nope."

"Well, if you somehow miraculously remember what happened, then give me a call. Here's my card." He reached in his back pocket and handed him his card.

"Hey Sanchez!" Tony Boy yelled, stopping him before he walked out of the room. "How's a white boy like you get a Mexican name like Sanchez?"

"My great grandfather was Hispanic. Now tell me how a yellow guy with a brown name gets beat blue?" Detective Sanchez counterattacked.

Tony Boy flipped him the middle finger as he walked out smiling. This whole situation was like a big puzzle and Tony Boy sat there in deep thought as he tried to piece everything together. Something just wasn't adding up right! And then like a bolt of lightning, it hit him. He pressed the button for the nurse so many times, he was for certain that he had broken it. Within 60 seconds, Capri came running in.

"Is everything alright?"

"Naw, it ain't, I need to get in touch with my niece A.S.A.P.!"

"You know you can use this phone whenever you want. Just give me her number and I'll dial it for you."

"It's 2 4 8 - 6 9 6 - 3 1 3 3."

"Okay, Mr. Brown it's ringing. Who should I ask to speak with?"

"Cassandra."

CHAPTER 15

"Why are you about to call Fred?" Cassandra asked suspiciously.

"Just come on and I'll tell you when we get inside," Nick said, rushing her into the apartment.

Cassandra thought that Nick was losing his mind. There was already one person that potentially wanted to kill them, but calling Fred would add several more to the list.

"What the fuck is going on, Nick?" Cassandra yelled as he closed the apartment door.

"Listen baby, I came up with a plan."

"Well, I'm waiting to hear it and sure in the fuck better be good!" She snapped with her arms folded as she sat on the sofa.

"Alright listen, I'm gone call Fred and tell him everything that happened—"

"Have you lost your fucking mind?!" Cassandra interrupted. "Why the fuck would you call Fred?"

"Because Nate is gone kill us both!" Nick shouted. "After we do this shit, he's gone kill us both and you know it! The only way we gone stay alive is if we kill him first and I have the perfect plan."

"Nigga, if you tell Fred that we trying to rob him, then he gone kill all four of us!" Cassandra yelled, still appalled at Nick's idiotic plan.

"Got damn, just let me finish before you get to jumping to conclusions! You haven't even heard the plan yet," Nick pleaded.

"Okay, I'm listening." Cassandra said as she began to tap her right Gucci sneaker on the floor, while simultaneously twirling the two-carat diamond stud in her ear.

"Listen baby, I'ma call Fred and tell him everything that happened. I'ma let him know that this whole thing was all Nate's doings. I'ma tell him that I'm calling because I don't have anywhere else to turn to. Nate is trying to drag us along to do some bullshit and we don't want no parts in it. You know Fred looks at me like I'm his little brother; so I'ma play the little brother role. Now, by me calling and giving him a heads-up, two things are guaranteed to happen. For one, he's gone kill Nate, and for two, it's going to make us closer. That's gone put me right into his immediate circle, and before you know it, we'll be rich."

"But what about Shardae?"

"What about her?" Nick asked with a "fuck Shardae" look on his face.

"Naw, that's my sister and I'm not about to let nothing happen to her. Why can't we just kill Nate after he kills Fred?"

"Naw, it ain't gone work like that."

"It will work 'cause I'll help. I got yo' back, babe."

"Naw, you gotta just trust me on this one, San. Nothing is going to happen to Shardae. Fred is in love with that girl, and you know I'm not gone let nothing happen to us, right?"

"Yeah, I know," Cassandra said nonchalantly.

"Do you trust me?" Nick asked, starting to sound repetitive.

"Yes," Cassandra said with an attitude as she inhaled deeply and slowly exhaled, letting Nick know that she didn't wish to continue to talk to him.

Sensing the growing tension in the room, Nick walked over to Cassandra and gently grabbed her face. He placed a soft kiss on her lips. The kiss just so happened to be exactly what she needed to put her at ease. She knew that Nick wasn't the toughest man in the world, but he somehow managed to make her feel indispensable at the right moments.

"San, I love you."

"I love you too, baby," Cassandra replied as she leaned up for another kiss. "Hurry up and call Fred so we can't get this shit over with."

Nick reached into his pocket to grab his phone and dialed Fred's number.

"Hello," Fred answered on the third ring.

"What's up bro?"

"What's up dog, you alright?"

"Naw bro, I ain't alright. I gotta problem and I need some help. This nigga Nate—"

"Whoa! Whoa! We not going to discuss any of our problems over the phone. You feel me?" Fred said, cutting Nick off in mid-sentence.

"So what should I—"

Fred cut him off again. "Where you at?"

"I'm at home."

"Well meet me at the Five Guys on Michigan Street. I'll be there in 30 minutes."

"Alright bro; I'm on my way."

Nick couldn't help but to crack a smile when he hung up the phone. He was excited at the fact that Fred was receptive about meeting with him. As far he was concerned, this was perfect.

"What'd he say?" Cassandra asked.

"I'm about to go and meet him right now." Nick said as he grabbed her car keys off the kitchen table. "I'll be right back."

He kissed her on her forehead and walked out of the door. Cassandra was happy that Nick was becoming more astute, but he was still acting cowardly. She couldn't understand how he was afraid of someone that she wasn't even scared of. And the fact that one of Nick's main objectives was to get into Fred's circle also wasn't sitting too well with her. As far as she was concerned, they didn't need Fred because if push came to shove, she'd kill him herself. Suddenly, her train of thought was broken by her ringing cell phone. She was puzzled as she looked at the unknown number, but decided to still answer it anyways.

"Hello."

"Hi, I'm Capri at St. Paul Hospital. May I speak with Cassandra?"

"This is she."

"Well Cassandra, I'm here with your Uncle Tony and—"

"Oh my God! Is everything alright?" Cassandra asked frantically.

"Actually he's right here, so I'll let you talk to him," Capri said as she handed him the phone.

"Uncle Tony Boy?" Cassandra called.

"Hey Bay Girl," Tony Boy answered.

"What happened? Is everything alright?"

"Listen Bay Girl, I ain't gone do too much talkin' on this phone, ya dig? So I need you to get up here immejietely so we can talk. Where's Lil' Nicky?"

"He just left out, but what's going on? Are you okay?"

"Listen Bay Girl, I need you to hurry up and get up here. But you can't let nobody know that we talked. Not Lil' Nicky, not nobody! It's a bunch of shit that's goin' down, so hurry up and get here."

"Okay, I'm on my way. I'm leaving out the door right now. What room are you in?"

"I'm in room 224," Tony Boy answered as he read the numbers off the door.

"I'll be there in five minutes, Uncle Tony Boy."

"Okay, bye."

Fred was anxious to see what Nick wanted to talk about. But it really didn't matter because no matter what he said, he was still going to die. Whether minuscule or majuscule, he knew that Nick played a role in everything that was going on. And the bottom line was that he was going to have to pay the consequence. Fred walked in the restaurant and didn't see Nick, so he decided to take a seat. He sat at a table in the back of the restaurant that was furthest from the door so that he could see everything. Nick walked in about two minutes later. He spotted Fred and sat across from him at the table.

"What's up bro?" Nick said as he shook Fred's hand.

"All man, it ain't nothing. So uh, what's up with this lil' problem you got?" Fred requested trying to get straight to the point.

"The problem is Nate, bro. This nigga done went crazy."

"Oh yeah, what did he do?"

"Bro, the nigga killed Tony Boy," Nick whispered as he leaned forward, getting closer to Fred so he could hear him.

"What?! Why the fuck would he do that?!" Fred asked indignantly.

"Bro, that's just the half of it. Listen, I met him over Tony Boy's house right after I met you. When I got there, it was just Butch and Nate cause he had sent Tony Boy to the store."

"What Butch? Crackhead ass Butch?" Fred interrupted.

"Yeah, dat Butch." Nick continued. "So anyways, right after you called me, Tony Boy burst through the door talkin' bout the police was coming. So when I looked out the window and saw all the police cars, I panicked. I put all four bricks on the stove and burned 'em up."

"What?! You burned up the dope?! All man!" Fred interrupted flabbergasted by the whole incident.

"But hold on, this the killin' part. After they kick in the door and arrest Butch, they leave."

"What?" Fred asked trying to piece together the story.

"They just left," Nick reiterated, slapping his fist on the table. "After that, Nate started trippin'. He started going off on Tony Boy and then he pistol whipped him. Then he took a butcher knife and stabbed him about 20 times. Bro, it was blood everywhere. That shit looked like a scene from The First 48."

"How come you didn't stop him?"

"I did, but he hit me with the pistol and said that he'd kill me. You see my face, don't you?" Nick said, pointing to his swollen jaw.

"So what you wanna do, dog?"

"Listen bro, Nate is planning on robbing and killing you tonight. He made Shardae and San call you and come to the party last night. It was all a set-up, bro. He just needed to know where you stayed at. So when you pick up Shardae and San tonight, we supposed to already be waiting on y'all."

"So who's all supposed to be in on this?" Fred asked.

"It's just me, Nate and the girls. But you already know that we like brothers; that's why I'm coming to you like this in the first place. This nigga Nate gotta go and I don't have nowhere else to turn to. So whatever you need me to do bro, I'm wit you 100 percent. All I ask in return is that you help me get back on my feet. I lost everything and you know I'm a real ass nigga—"

"Listen, dog." Fred interrupted, cutting his speech short. "I got you. I'ma make sure I look out for you just like you looked out for me. Just stick to y'all same plan and I'll handle the rest from there. Does anybody know that you came to meet me?"

"Nope."

"So nobody knows that we just had this conversation?"

"Nope, nobody."

"Okay, and make sure you keep it like that. This conversation can't leave this table."

"Fa sho, bro."

"I gotta go and take care of some shit, so I'll see you later on tonight. Make sure y'all follow the same plan and remember, we never spoke today," Fred said as he stood up from the table and pulled a wad of hundred-dollar bills from his pocket. "Lunch on me." Fred said as he threw a hundred-dollar bill on the table.

"Good lookin, bro," Nick said as he shook Fred's hand.

Fred walked out of the restaurant in disbelief of how much a snake Nick was. He didn't believe Nick's story and as far as he was concerned; Nick, Nate, Cassandra and Shardae were all good as dead. Their demise was only a phone call away. Fred's train of thought was broken by his ringing cell phone.

"Fuck!" He yelled out to himself as he saw that it was Maria calling. She was supposed to be flying in from Atlanta today and he had completely forgot. Fred had too much shit going on, which made it far too dangerous for her to come and see him now. He dreaded having to cancel on her cause he knew how crazy she could get, but at this point, it was what it was.

"What's up baby?" Fred answered.

"Hi honey! Listen, you have to pick me up from the airport at 9 o'clock, okay?"

"Listen baby," Fred tried to interrupt.

"No, you listen." Maria cut him off. "I booked us a presidential suite at the W for two days, so you're all mine for the next 48 hours."

"Listen baby, right now really isn't the best time for you to come," Fred said, scratching his head waiting on a response.

"But babe, I already paid for the room and my flight is booked. Are you fucking serious?"

"I know. I'm so sorry, baby. Whatever you spent, I'll double it and give it back to you. And you have my word that next week, I'm going to make it all up to you. I promise."

"Next week, Fred? Next fucking week? Are you fucking kidding me?! You know what? I am sick and tired of you treating me like I'm some side bitch! This is the second time in a row that you've stood me up! Fuck you, Fred! Fuck you!" Maria screamed furiously as she hung up in his face.

Fred tried to call her back twice and didn't get an answer. But right now, he didn't have time to play phone tag. He had a much more important call to make. He pulled out his phone and dialed away.

"Yeah," Captain McGraw answered on the third ring.

"I need you to meet me at the spot, ASAP. It's important."

"Got dammit, I'll be there in a hour."

"Make it 30 minutes," Fred said as he hung up the phone.

CHAPTER 16

Cassandra was very anxious to find out what was going on with her uncle. Not only was she extremely tired, but she was beginning to become overwhelmed with all of what was going on. Her sleep deprivation had her feeling completely depleted. All she kept hoping was that she didn't have to kill anyone about her uncle. She knew that her uncle got high, but she also knew that he hustled, so she figured that he probably jacked off someone's dope or money and they decided to beat him up. Either way, she was riding with her uncle, right or wrong. Her eyes began to perspire like active armpits as she walked into room 224 and took a glimpse of her uncle.

"Oh my God, Uncle! Uncle Tony Boy, what happened?" Cassandra asked teary eyed as she grabbed his hand.

"I'm alright Bay Girl; I'm fine. Now I need you to be strong and wipe them tears. The shit done hit the fan and we ain't got no time to be crying."

It took a minute for Cassandra to get herself together. She wiped the tears from her eyes and took a deep breath.

"What happened Uncle Tony?"

"A few days ago, Lil' Nicky came by the house as mad as a junkyard dog. He said that him and Nate had been fightin' and something about him not likin Freddie and some other bullshit. So Lil' Nicky asked me was there a way to kill somebody and get away with it. Now I know the boy ain't no killa, it ain't in his blood. So I told him the next best thing, ya dig."

"So what did you tell him?" Cassandra interrupted.

"I told him the same thang that I always told you. You ain't got to necessarily gotta kill a nigga for him to die cause you can always trick a nigga into killing somebody or into getting they mothafuckin' self killed, ya dig? So he asked me how and I told him. If you want Nate dead, all you gotta do is tell a nigga like Freddie that Nate talkin' bout doin' something to him and see if he don't have that nigga smoked like a cigarette. If you want Freddie dead, then the next time you meet him to get that dope, cut it first and then take it to Nate and see if he don't kill that nigga. So the next day, I'm at the house wit' my main man Butch ya dig, and Nicky called saying that they was on they way to come and cook some shit. Now, normally they want me there by myself, but for some reason, this time Nicky told me to make sure Butch stayed—"

"What Butch?" Cassandra interrupted. "Crack head ass Butch from around the corner?"

"Well naw, he ain't really no crackhead, but he will smoke a rock every now and then, but that's my main man. But anyways, Nate pulls up first and sends me to the store. So I jump on the bike and who do I see on the next street in Mrs. Pope and thems driveway?"

"Who?"

"Lil' Nicky. Fred was pulling off in a big ass white truck and I saw Nicky put a duffle bag in his trunk and take another bag out. Now I was wondering what the fuck was going on, but I kept on pushing, ya dig, and he ain't even see me," Tony Boy explained. "Now on my way back from the store, I see nothing but police cars coming up the street, so I hurry back to the house to give the boys a heads-up. So when I run in and tell them the police is comin', Nicky cuts on all four eyes on the stove and burns up all the dope. All four kilos! The police buss in the door ya dig, and arrest Butch and leave right back out," Tony Boy continued. "But by that time, all the dope had burned up. That's how I knew the dope was fake, ya dig. Don't no dope burn up that fast. After that, Nate started acting a damn fool. He pulled a pistol out on Nicky and told him that he was gone set up Freddie to rob him. Then the hoe bitch cold cocked the shit out of me and knocked me out and stabbed me all in the stomach."

"Oh my God!" Cassandra gasped, placing both of her hands over her mouth in utter disbelief.

"Lil' Nicky did all of this bullshit!" Tony Boy shouted belligerently. "Then this punk ass police officer comes to question me, talkin' bout they received a anonymous call from Mrs. Pope and them's house sayin' I was hoardin' a fugitive 'cause I had Butch over."

"What?" Cassandra asked, still puzzled as she tried to piece everything together.

"Yeah, and I told you that I saw Lil' Nicky's bitch ass over at her house. And he the one who told me to make sure I had Butch over. Boy, I swear that lil' nigga is slick as wet baby oil."

"Uncle Tony, what color was the bag that you saw Nick putting in the trunk?"

"He put some kind of shopping bag in the trunk and took out a red duffle bag—"

"Are you sure the bag was red?" Cassandra interrupted before he could finish.

"Yeah, it was a red duffle bag," Tony Boy reiterated.

Everything was starting to make sense now. The red duffle bag was the same bag that Nick had on their living room floor. When she mentioned the bag, Nick quickly moved it and changed the subject. Then he was so adamant about making a side deal with Fred just to kill Nate. Nick wasn't that timid after all. In fact, he was much more sagacious than anyone had ever given him credit for. He somehow managed to manipulate everyone and use them as mere mules with menial roles in his intricate, yet sinister plan to have Nate killed after stealing all of his money. It took more than just bold courage for Nick to attempt to pull off what he had just tried to do. And if Tony Boy would have died, then his plan just might have worked.

"What should I do, Uncle Tony Boy?"

"You should get the fuck from 'round here. That's what you need to do, Bay Girl. It's 'bout to be a whole lotta bloodshed, and I don't want you nowhere round it. You need to get Shardae and that pistol I gave you for Christmas and go somewhere and chill out for a few weeks."

"But what about Nick and Nate? And what about Fred?"

"Motha fuck Nicky, Nate and Fred! Them niggas like some wild pit bull puppies; they gone take care of each other."

"But Uncle Tony, look what they did to you!" Cassandra protested.

"You stay out of this, Bay Girl. Let them niggas take care of each other. Now promise me that you gone stay out of this shit."

"I promise, Uncle Tony," Cassandra replied before pouting and smacking her lips.

"Now go and get Shardae and a gun and get the hell on somewhere. Now go on and get out of here."

"Okay; I love you, Uncle Tony," Cassandra said as she kissed him on the cheek.

"Love you too, Bay Girl. Now go on and get out of here!"

Despite her promise to her uncle, she was definitely going to get involved. But first, she had to get back to the apartment before Nick did.

Nate was getting prepared for war. If he wasn't anything else, he was always combat ready. He had bulletproof vests, night-vision binoculars, and all types of other artillery laid across his bed like a new outfit in the first day of school. Lying next to the bulletproof vest were two .40 glocks, an Uzi, and a hunting knife with an eight-inch blade. For an average person, that may have been too much to take to a robbery, but not for Nate. He had every intention to take every weapon that was on the bed with him. This was the type of stuff that Nate lived for.

The chaotic part of the streets is what gave him a rush, but this one felt a little different. The closer they came to robbing and killing Fred, the more paranoid he became. He had been longing to kill Fred for years, so that wasn't what he was paranoid about. It was Nick. Lately, Nick had a certain aura about himself and it wasn't sitting well with Nate at all. Not only had he served time in prison, but he had been in the streets all his life, so he was very good at reading people. He knew that something was up with Nick; he just couldn't quite put his finger on it.

Long ago he was taught that it's better to be safe than sorry. And he loved living too much to be sorry. So after they got the money, he was going to kill Nick just to be safe. He would have to try his best to make it look like it was an accident or else. He knew he'd have to kill Cassandra as well. Either way was cool with him. He had made his mind up and that's how it was going to go down. Now, all he had to do was plant the seed in Shardae's brain.

"Shardae!" Nate yelled. "Shardae!"

Shardae was knocked out on the living room sofa and wasn't hearing a word that he was saying. Unbeknownst to Nate, she had been up all night, doing drugs and having sex. She got maybe three good hours of sleep, allowing the exhaustion to take over her body.

"Shardae!" Nate yelled again as he smacked her on the butt.

The burning sensation of the slap woke her up instantly. She had been in such a deep sleep that she hadn't heard a word that Nate said. All she felt was the slap. With her already having a guilty conscience from last night, she automatically assumed that Nate wanted to have sex. She was far too sore and wore out to have sex, so she came up with the most feasible excuse that every woman says when they don't want to copulate.

"Nate stop; I'm bleeding."

"Girl, sit up. We gotta talk."

"About what?" Shardae asked, yawning as she sat up and stretched.

"Look baby, you my girl and I love you. And I want to be completely honest with you and—"

"What happened?" Shardae interrupted, wishing that he would skip the preamble and tell her what was going on.

"Okay, listen. Nick killed Tony Boy."

Shardae's jaws dropped as her brain registered the new information. She gasped and covered her mouth with both of her hands. "Oh my God! Does San know?"

"Naw. You, me and Nick are the only ones that know."

"Oh my God, Nate! What happened?"

"After we found out the dope was fake, Nick started trippin'. Tony Boy said something to him and he just snapped. He picked up a knife and started stabbing him."

Tears begin to roll down Shardae's cheeks like rain on a windshield. Tony Boy was her best friend's uncle and he was dead. But for some reason, the story just wasn't adding up. Nick wasn't the killing type, and why would he kill his girlfriend's uncle? None of this was making any sense.

"Just like that? He just killed him, just like that?" Shardae asked trying to piece together the story.

"The nigga had been doing lines of powder and just snapped out. He was upset and it was almost like he had something to prove. And who better for him to take his aggression out on than a crackhead?"

"You couldn't stop him or nothing?" Shardae asked still crying.

"I tried to, but it was too late," Nate replied trying his hardest to convince her of his lies.

"So what now?"

"We gone have to stick to our same plan for tonight. But when this whole Tony Boy situation surfaces and Nick don't own up to what the fuck he did, then I'ma kill him. I'm not going down for nothing that I ain't do." Nate looked Shardae directly in her eyes. "So are you wit' me or what?"

Shardae took a deep breath before looking back up at him. "You know I'm with you."

"That's my girl," Nate said smiling as he kissed her on the forehead.

Shardae knew that danger was imminent. She knew that none of this was going to sit well with her best friend. Cassandra would definitely retaliate for someone killing her uncle. Shardae was just hoping that Nate didn't have anything to do with it. And despite his earnest attempt to convince her, she knew that his story was mendacious. The only thing was she couldn't prove it, but the truth would soon come to light.

CHAPTER 17

The rain was pouring down at a rapid speed as thunder and lightning began to strike. The sounds of the weather would put you under the impression that they were bowling in heaven. Mother Nature must've been pissed off this particular night. Fred pulled his truck into the back of an abandoned warehouse, and awaiting his arrival was a navy Ford Crown Victoria. This was the spot where he normally met Captain McGraw whenever he needed some dirty work done. Captain McGraw got out of his car, wearing a cheap suit with a newspaper covering his head from the rain. He being out of shape was really starting to show as he struggled to get into the truck.

"Now what's so got damn important that I have to leave from the dinner table with my wife on our anniversary?! I'll be getting my ass chewed out for at least a month for this," Captain McGraw complained as slammed the door of the dually truck.

"We gotta problem on our hands and when it's over with, you'll be able to buy her something nice enough to forget about the anniversary," Fred said as he reached into the center console and grabbed a wad of cash that was wrapped in rubber bands.

"Okay, so what the fuck is going on?" McGraw asked impatiently.

"I need you to kill two birds with one stone. Here's 15," Fred handed him 150 one hundred-dollar bills. "I'll give you the rest when I read about it in the newspaper."

"Who are they and how much time do I got?"

"It's Nathaniel Lowe and Nicholas Wright, and I need it done yesterday."

"Yesterday?!"

"Yeah, yesterday. They should be both on their way to try and kill me in the next couple hours, so you'll have to intercept them before they get to my house."

"Got dammit, Fred! You somehow always manage to stay in some shit. I can't keep putting my ass on the line like this. Now, I'll see what I can do, but I ain't making no promises."

"See what you can do? I'm not trying to hear that shit! You have to do it!"

"Now, you just wait a got damn minute! Since when did I start taking orders from you?"

"Since I started paying you. I don't work for you! You work for me and you know exactly what the fuck you signed up for," Fred retorted. "Now I just told you them mothafuckas are on their way to kill me! And I don't want to hear any of that bullshit about yo' ass being on the line cause with all the crooked shit you do in the city, your ass stays on the line. Save the lectures for your kids and just do what the fuck I'm paying you to do!" Fred snapped.

"I'm gonna do it this time got dammit, but this'll be the last time I do this without a 72-hour heads up. You got it?!"

"Well, the next time I find out some mothafuckas wanna kill me, I'll just tell them to give me a 72-hour notice. That way I can call and give you a heads up," Fred said facetiously.

"I'm not fucking around got dammit; this will be the last fucking time!"

"Alright man, go on and get out of my truck so you can take care of your business 'cause the clock is ticking. I'll call you in the morning after I watch the 7 o'clock news."

"You're a real fucking asshole jerk, you know that?" Captain McGraw said as he got out of the truck.

Captain McGraw hated the fact that Fred always gave him so much to do in so little time. He had approximately two hours to kill two different people, and he didn't know where either of them were. Not to mention, today was the night of his 25th anniversary. He could really use the extra cash and even if he couldn't, Fred didn't give him much of a choice. Captain McGraw was definitely going to need some help and it was only one person who he could trust. He dialed the number and prayed he got an answer.

"Hello."

"Sanchez, it's me. Listen, I need you to get ahold of Nathaniel Wright and Nicholas Jones immediately. I want you to go to Nate's house first and I'm in route now," Captain McGraw ordered.

"Did you already call for back up?" Detective Sanchez asked.

"No, I didn't call for any got damn back up. We are the back up. Just do what I tell you Sanchez, you'll get an early Christmas bonus in the morning. Now hurry!"

"Alright, I'll be there in 20 minutes."

After leaving the hospital, Cassandra rushed to get back to their apartment. As the rain continued to pour, it was evident that the weather wasn't on her side. She weaved in and out of traffic, trying her hardest not to get into an accident as her car began to mimic a hydroplane. The windshield wipers were moving so fast that at one point, she thought they were going to break off. It was imperative that she make it home before Nick.

She believed everything that her uncle told her, but it was one thing that she had to check out for herself. And that one thing would solidify everything. As she pulled into the apartment complex, she could see that Nick still hadn't arrived, so she knew that time was of the essence because he'd be pulling up at any minute. She rushed in the house to get Nick's car keys and naturally, they were nowhere to be found. She looked on the kitchen table, on top of the refrigerator and on the kitchen counter and found nothing. She looked on the coffee table, in the bathroom and on the floor and found nothing. Then right in plain view on the sofa were the car keys. They must've fell out of his pocket when he sat down. She shot back outside and hit the trunk button on the keys.

Everything began to set in as soon as her eyes made contact with the Foot Locker shopping bag that sat in the trunk. She looked inside the bag and it was what looked to be four kilos of dope wrapped in silver electrical tape. Everything made perfect sense now. Nick had done everything that Tony Boy had accused him of. Now all she had to do was call Shardae and let her know exactly what was going on. Before she could get her cell phone out, she saw Nick pulling into the complex. She ran back into the apartment, praying that he didn't see her. It was no time to call Shardae now, so she did the next best thing and sent a text.

The day was getting more and more sluggish as every minute went past. The pouring rain and thunder were loud enough to wake up a hibernating bear. Nate thought this was the perfect night to pull off a murder and robbery. Mother Nature was definitely on his side. Nate paced back and forth across the living room floor, stopping on occasion only to briefly look out of the window. Nick and Cassandra were late and it was beginning to drive him crazy. Not only were their tardiness making him extremely impatient, but he was now starting to draw suspicion. This was the very reason he didn't want to let them out of his sight in the first place. He decided to call and see what was taking so long.

"What's up bro?" Nick answered on the first ring.

"Man, where da the fuck are y'all at?!" Nate asked aggressively.

"We'll be pulling up in five minutes."

"Alright man, hurry up!" Nate snapped as he hung up the phone.

Shardae was very nervous about tonight. Just thinking about what they were about to do had her guts rumbling. She was sitting on the toilet when her phone begin to vibrate on the vanity. It was a text message from Cassandra. Reading the message made her even more nervous. The massage read:

When we were in school we vowed to always trust each other no matter who or what. A lot of shit done happened over the past 2 days that we didn't know nothing about. Tonight I just need u to trust me and follow my lead. I love you

Shardae didn't know what to make of the text and time wasn't on her side because as soon as she stepped out of the bathroom, Nick and Cassandra were standing in the living room.

CHAPTER 18

Fred was standing at the island in his kitchen with a kilo of cocaine on the granite countertop. After pulling out his Swiss Army pocket knife, he made a small incision into the silver electrical tape that the kilo was wrapped in. He then took the knife and began to break off small pieces of the block chopping them until they turned into dust. When he finished, he had three small lines of cocaine. Before he could bend his face down to ingest one, his phone begin to ring.

"Hello," Fred answered not even looking at the number.

"Hey, it's me," The female voice answered.

"Look, right now isn't a good time to talk," Fred said, recognizing who the voice belonged to.

"But we really need to talk. I have something very important to tell you. I—"

"Look, I told you right now isn't a good time. Plus, I got dog here with me right now. I'll call you later."

"Okay, bye," The voice on the other end said before Fred hung up the phone.

Fred didn't have a clue as to what she wanted to tell him. But right now, he didn't care. He had more important things to worry about. He bent down and snorted all three lines back to back.

"Wuz dat dem, main?" Diego asked as he walked from the back room, handing Fred a bulletproof vest.

"Naw, that wasn't nobody," Fred said as he quickly put his phone back in his pocket.

"You betta slow down main. You know we got beenis on the flo," Diego warned.

"I'm straight dog, I'm straight. I'm 'bout to call ol' girl and them and see if they ready," Fred said as he pulled out his phone and dialed Cassandra's number.

"Hello," Cassandra answered on the second ring.

"What's up? Y'all ready for me to come and get y'all?"

"Yeah, we was just about to call you. Are you coming to pick us up now?"

"Yeah. Where y'all at?"

"We at Day house. Do you know where it's at?"

"Yeah, I'm on my way," Fred said on his way out the door.

Fred put on his bulletproof vest and zipped his hoodie up over it. The effects of the cocaine had kicked in and he was feeling focused. He cocked back his P89 .45 Ruger before putting it on his hip and grabbed his car keys.

"I'll be right back, dog; so, be ready," Fred said on his way out the door.

"I stay ready, main," Diego said smiling exposing his mouth full of gold.

Nate looked like he was a part of an SWAT team that was about to raid the jungle. He had on a pair of camouflage pants with the matching camouflage twin .40 glocks. The twin pistols were on a holster that was attached to the bulletproof vest that covered his torso.

His black leather gloves accentuated what he had on, giving him a true villain look.

"Man, we gotta hurry up and leave now so we can beat 'em there," Nate said to Nick as he cocked both of his pistols and put them back in the holster.

Although not dressed for the part as strong as Nate was, Nick too was combat ready. He had on a bullet proof vest under his T-shirt with a pistol on his hip.

They got the address to Fred's house from the girls, kissed them, and headed out the door. Their plan was to already be at Fred's house before him and the girls even got there. The element of surprise was their main advantage, or so they thought.

So far, the car ride was quiet. Neither of them had even bothered to cut the radio on. They were both in deep thought as to what was about to go down. For Nate, this was a walk in the park. It would be like taking candy from a baby. He loved the rush that he got from all the drama more than he loved the actual drama. Nick, on the other hand, was nervous and excited at the same time. In his eyes, he was minutes away from executing one of the shrewdest plans ever concocted by man. Then all of a sudden both of their emotions were extremely intensified. As their car turned onto the next street, their lives along with their million-dollar expectations and aspirations flashed before their eyes. The absolute worst-case scenario has just happened. Just that quick in the blink of an eye, in the turn of a corner, both men became victims of circumstances. An unmarked navy blue Tahoe truck got behind them and cut the siren on. They were being pulled over.

He picked up his cell phone and called Captain McGraw as Nick and Nate's car pulled to the shoulder of the road.

"Hey, it's me Sanchez. I got 'em."

Shardae was anxious to find out what was really going on, so she was relieved to finally see Nick and Nate leave. Now, she could finally ask Cassandra some questions about Tony Boy and about the strange text message that she sent her. She had a multitude of thoughts and emotions going through her body and she needed some answers.

"Girl, please tell me what the hell is going on!" Shardae demanded as soon as Nick and Nate pulled off.

Before Cassandra could even get a word out, they both were startled by a beeping horn. The sounds coming from outside emulated a Mack truck. Shardae peeked through the curtains and to her surprise, it was Fred.

"Shit! It's Fred!" Shardae yelled in disappointment knowing she wouldn't be able to get the full story

"Listen Day Day, we don't have no time for me to explain everything, so just follow my lead and trust me in this one. I'm not gone let nothing happen to us. Here, put this in your purse," Cassandra said as she cocked and handed her a 9mm pistol that was small enough to fit in a Timberland boot. "You might need it."

Shardae put the pistol in her purse and they walked out the house and got in the truck with Fred.

CHAPTER 19

"Where the hell are you?" Captain McGraw asked.

"I'm on Evelyn Street between Tracy and Edgewood. I've got 'em pulled over right now."

"Sanchez, you stay put, ya hear me? Just stay put and I'll be there in five minutes. Do not let them get away!" Captain McGraw ordered.

"Alright, Cap."

The sound of sirens and flashing lights behind them almost made Nick urinate on himself. He was seriously about to have a panic attack. It seemed as if his very

well-thought-out plan was about to go to shambles. He was in complete disbelief that this was happening. Not only did they have enough weapons to go to war with a small country, but Nate had just lit a blunt, and the smell of weed would give the police probable cause to search the vehicle.

"Look man, just be cool. We don't even know what they pulling us over for. We legit so we straight," Nate said in hopes of relaxing Nick.

As Detective Sanchez approached their car, Nate rolled down his window to see what the problem was. Sanchez twisted his face at the marijuana stench coming from the vehicle. Before he could even get out a word, Nick fired two shots from his pistol hitting Sanchez in the torso. He dropped to the ground as the bullets pierced his chest.

"Man, what the fuck is you doin?!" Nate yelled in disbelief.

Before Nick could respond, Nate opened up the driver side door and fired four more shots into Detective Sanchez's back as he tried crawling back to the truck. Nate closed his door back and sped away.

"I had to, bro. I had to do it!" Nick pleaded "If I wouldn't a did that, we'd a been fucked!"

"Damn, nigga! Damn! That was some G shit!" Nate screamed ecstatically as he began to punch the steering wheel. "It ain't no turning back for us now. That's what the fuck I'm talking about!"

Adrenaline was rushing through both of their bodies at a high velocity. As Nate looked at Nick, he had a smile on his face from ear to ear. Was it the lines of cocaine that they were doing before they left the house that gave Nick this sudden burst of courage? Or was it the weed that they were smoking? Or had Nick just been a killer all along? All of these thoughts were running through Nate's mind. But one thing he knew for certain was that when all of this was over, he was definitely going to have to kill Nick before he exercised the thought of killing him.

The weather in Southern California was beautiful. Carlos sat at the edge of his infinity swimming pool which sat outside of his 3,500 square foot home. He wore beige linen pants rolled up to his knees to prevent them from getting wet as his feet soaked in the pool. The top four buttons of his shirt were unfastened exposing a small gold necklace that was entangled in his chest hairs. He sat puffing on his $100 cigar trying to calm his nerves. His patience with Fred was beginning to wear very thin. It seemed as if Fred was trying to dodge him.

He had just sent Fred a shipment of 30 kilos and had yet to receive a dime. The deal was Fred was supposed to send the first $225,000 within the first 24 hours of receiving the shipment, and the second $225,000 when he got finished. Carlos was upset and starting to get worried because he had been calling Fred all day and hadn't gotten an answer. He didn't want to get his niece involved but at this point, he didn't have a choice. Fred was into him for almost a half of a million dollars and he knew that if anyone could get in touch with him, that it would be his niece, Maria. He decided to give her a call.

"Hello," Maria answered on the first ring, hoping it was Fred.

"Hello sweetheart. How is my favorite niece doing?"

"I'm doing okay, but I'm kinda in the middle of something, Uncle Carlos. Can I call you back?"

"I just wanted to know if you had heard from Fred. I'm kind of worried cause he's owes me money and he's not answering my phone calls."

"You know what Uncle Carlos, his phone is broke," Maria lied.

"His phone is broken?" Carlos asked making sure he had heard her correctly.

"Yeah, he dropped it in some water. He supposed to get a new one tomorrow."

"Well, as soon as you talk to him, make sure he calls me."

"Okay Uncle Carlos, I will."

"Okay, good bye, sweetheart."

"Bye."

Maria's day seemed to be getting worse as the hours went by. She had just lied to her uncle about Fred having a broken phone because she sensed that he may be in some deep water. The two aspirin she took were just now starting to kick in. The medicine's temporary relief of symptoms made it to where she now has 99 problems and a migraine headache wasn't one of them. Her exhaustion was just now starting to overpower her feeling of antipathy towards Fred. Despite her being in love with him, right now she hated him. It had been hours since their argument and she had called him at least 10 times without getting an answer. But at this point, she didn't really care, because she had a surprise for him. She was just now arriving at the airport from a two-hour flight from Atlanta. Her plane ticket and room at the W had already been paid for so she decided to still go to Michigan and pop up on Fred. She kind of figured that Fred was seeing other women due to their long-distance relationship, but this time was different.

In her eyes, Fred had gotten too comfortable and now his infidelity seemed blatant. She felt as if Fred didn't care anymore and his actions were beginning to show it. But she had something for that. This surprise visit would definitely fix that. But before going to Fred's house, she had to pick up her girl, Capri. Once Capri found out that it was a potential situation, she insisted that she tag along. And they both had every intention of making a scene, if need be. After picking up her luggage and rental car, she called Capri to let her know that she was on her way.

"What up girl?" Capri said answering her phone.

"Hey, I'm just leaving the airport and now I'm on my way to get you."

"Alright, I'm just about to get in the shower and change. I have to get out of these hospital scrubs."

"Well, you need to hurry 'cause I'll be there in 25 minutes"

"Okay, I'm hurrying."

"Okay bye," Maria said hanging up the phone.

Captain McGraw has his sirens on which enabled him to triple the legal speeding limit in his Crown Vic. In his eyes, Detective Sanchez was finally stepping up to the plate. At first, he didn't think that Sanchez was cut out for the job, but he was beginning to prove him wrong. In fact, he was so proud of Sanchez that he was going to give him his Christmas bonus tonight. As Captain McGraw bent the corner, he could see a lifeless body lying next to Detective Sanchez's truck. The closer he got, he could see that the lifeless body was Detective Sanchez. He jumped out of the Crown Vic to see if he was okay.

"Sanchez! Sanchez! Don't you leave here, got dammit!" Captain McGraw yelled as he checked the detective for a pulse.

Detective Sanchez was still breathing, but he was starting to hemorrhage. Captain McGraw hopped in his truck and called for an ambulance.

"I got an officer down! I repeat, I got an officer down! Send an ambulance immediately!" Captain McGraw yelled through the radio.

"State your location," The dispatcher ordered.

Captain McGraw watched helplessly as blood profusely poured out of Sanchez mimicking a water fountain.

"Got dammit! Don't you leave here, Sanchez!" Captain McGraw yelled.

But it was too late. Sanchez had just taken his last breath. He didn't want to leave him like this, but at this point it was nothing he could do. Sanchez was gone and if he didn't get to Nick and Nate before they got to Fred, then he'd be gone too. He jumped back into his car and rushed to Fred's house, leaving Sanchez dead on the side of the road.

CHAPTER 20

It was raining cats and dogs. The rain was coming down so hard that just by listening to it sounded like hail. With the exception of a few porch lights, the street was completely dark. As Fred crept down the block in the big dually truck, his headlights lit up the entire cul-de-sac. His plan was for him and Diego to have their way with the girls before disposing them. Then first thing tomorrow morning, he'd call Carlos and buy a little more time so he could get the rest of his money together. He still had plenty of dope, he just didn't have all of the money. The sudden threat of his life had hindered his hustling ability quite a bit. But by this time tomorrow, he'd have everything under control. Right now, Nick and Nate were the furthest thing from his mind. He wasn't at all concerned about them; in fact, he was pretty sure that by now they were both dead. He and Captain McGraw had be doing business like this for years, so he knew that Nick and

Nate would be a piece of cake. Fred pulled into the two-car garage and cut the truck off.

"Let's get this party started," Fred said jokingly as he got out of the truck.

Before he could close the door of the truck, he was blindsided with a blow to the head from the .40 Glock of a masked gunman. He fell to the ground not knowing what hit him until the sound of the bullet being loaded into the chamber of the pistol gave him confirmation.

He could feel the cold steel of the barrel pressing the back of his head.

"Get yo bitch ass up, nigga!" the masked gunman ordered.

As he got up, he and the girls were warned to be quiet by another man who also wore a mask brandishing a gun. They were all ordered to walk in the house with the masked gunman accompanying them. Both men unveiled their masks as they walked into the foyer of the condo. Fred could not believe that Captain McGraw didn't take care of this situation. Right then, he made a promise to himself that if he made it out of this situation, he would personally kill Captain

McGraw. Fred pleaded for them not to kill him in hopes of tipping Diego off about the danger.

"C'mon man, don't kill me. Don't kill me, dog," Fred pleaded.

"Shut the fuck up!" Nate yelled as he whacked Fred across the back of the head again with his pistol. "Hit the lights, Nick."

As soon as Nick turned on the light switch, he was hit by the striking blow of a shotgun handle to his mouth. The blunt force of the shotgun knocked him to the ground along with three of his teeth. Saliva and tooth fragments flew through the air as Nick covered his mouth, screaming in agonizing pain.

"Chitch, chitch!" was the sound that hollered from the shotgun as Diego cocked it loading a slug into the chamber.

"Main, if you don't put dat mothafuckin' gun down, I'm a turn this nigga face to chitlings!" Diego ordered Nate as he held the shotgun to Nick's face.

"Fuck that nigga! Kill him!" Nate yelled.

Before Diego could even react to the comment, Fred broke loose from the collar grip that Nate had on him. He tried running to the other side of the pool table for cover, but it was too late. Nate had already started firing bullets in his direction. The first two shots hit the pool table, shattering it into a thousand pieces. Exotic fishes flopped around in the broken glass, gasping for air. Fred spun around as the third shot hit him in the back of his shoulder. Nate sent three more shots, two hitting Fred in the chest and one hitting him in the face, dropping him to the floor. Both Shardae and Cassandra began to scream and take cover as Diego started firing shots in an attempt to hit Nate.

"Bitch ass nigga!" Diego yelled as he continued to fire the weapon.

Nate was somehow able to dodge the slugs from the shotgun, but unable to elude the impending danger that stood behind him. Three bullets from a .45 hit the back of his head pushing pieces of his skull and brains through the front of his face. Shardae and Cassandra both screamed as Nate's body collapsed to the floor.

"Lower your weapon!" Captain McGraw ordered Diego. "I'm Captain McGraw; I'm here to help you and

Fred," Captain McGraw flashed his badge with his free hand while still pointing the .45 at Diego. As Diego lowered his weapon, Captain McGraw shot him three times in the chest, dropping him to the ground.

"Now you two bitches better tell me where that got damn money is right now!" Captain McGraw ordered with his .45 pointed in Shardae and Cassandra's direction.

"We don't know nothing about no money!" Cassandra pleaded.

"Boom!"

Captain McGraw's skilled marksmanship showed as he shot at Cassandra barely hitting her in the shoulder. Shardae and Cassandra both begin screaming like they had both been shot.

"It's just a flesh wound but the next one is gonna go right through that pretty little face of yours. Now tell me where that got damn money is!" Captain McGraw yelled as he begin to gently rub Cassandra's face with the back of his hand in a creepy way.

"I swear we don't know anything about no money. Please don't kill us," Cassandra pleaded.

"Alright that's it, got dammit!" Captain McGraw yelled.

Before Captain McGraw's brain could send the message telling his index finger to squeeze the trigger, his life came to an abrupt end. Through all of the deadly turmoil, Nick had somehow managed to keep his presence undetected as he killed Captain McGraw with a single shot to the temple.

"San, you alright?!" Nick asked frantically.

"Yeah, I'm fine."

"Alright we gotta get the fuck up outta here. San, hurry up and go grab the money!"

Shardae was still in shock by all the events that had just taken place. She stood in the corner sobbing as she looked at all the bodies on the floor. Nick hugged her in an endeavor to make her feel better.

"Shardae, the police are on their way. You gotta pull it together 'cause we gotta get the fuck up outta here."

Cassandra came back dragging two Louis Vuitton bags in each hand. Nick smiled as he saw the bags. This had worked out better than his original plan. Not only did he have the four kilos of cocaine, but they had all the money, too. Plus he had rid himself of Nate. He bent down to grab the bags from Cassandra and when he stood up, he was staring down the barrel of a loaded pink-handled chrome .38 special.

"What the fuck are you doing?" Nick asked in bewilderment.

"You know my uncle almost died, right? But you wouldn't know, 'cause you thought he was dead right? Or did you just not give a fuck?!" Cassandra shouted with the pistol still pointed in Nick's face.

"Baby, I swear to God I didn't have nothing to do with that. That was all Nate. But we rich now, baby. We can start a whole new life!" Nick pleaded.

Tears began to roll down Cassandra's cheeks as she stood there with the gun pointed at Nick's face. Nick was still pleading his case, but she wasn't hearing anything that he was saying. His words were going in one ear and out the other.

"Goodbye, Nick."

"But baby, baby, I swear to God baby!" Nick said as he started to cry.

"Boom!"

Cassandra pulled the trigger shooting Nick right between the eyes. As the bullet entered his cranium, he died before his body even hit the ground. Shardae was shocked at the turn of events. All the dead bodies on the floor made the living room look like a war zone. At this point, both Shardae and Cassandra were crying profusely. They shared a brief embrace with each other before Cassandra broke up the moment.

"Day, we gotta go. We gotta go!" Cassandra said, still sobbing.

They loaded the duffle bags of money into Fred's truck. Shardae got in the driver seat and they pulled out of the driveway. They could see the headlights from a car approaching as they drove down the cul-de-sac. The car began to slow down as they got closer. The other car stopped as they drove past. Shardae was able to make eye contact with who appeared to be a younger good-looking Hispanic woman. She was so caught up in the moment that she missed the dirty look given to her by the woman in the other vehicle.

"Where we goin?" Shardae asked.

"I don't know, Day Day; just drive."